THE GILDED STONE

DARK TIDES

BOOK FIVE

By
Candace Osmond

CANDACE OSMOND

Cover Work by Majeau Designs
Facebook.com/MajeauDesigns

DEDICATION

To Corey, my rock in this crazy world.

ACKNOWLEDGMENTS

I'm eternally grateful for my readers. Without them, I'd surely be nothing. And to my author bestie, JJ King. My partner in crime who always pushes me to "get it done".

And to my love, Corey. The mastermind behind the design of all my covers, illustrations, maps, merchandise, and the holder of my heart. Thank you for putting up with me.

CHAPTER ONE

How long can one live on the outside? I often wondered that, in times like these. Times where I found myself amongst the blaring noise of this new world while the inside of my head rang hollow. Empty. Lost.

The Siren's Call was filled with happy people as I leaned against one of the large entryways and watched our friends dance. The sound of overflowing mugs clanking the tables could be heard just under the surface of music and laughter. Fiddles and drums mixed with candlelight and ale.

A stone fireplace warmed the cloud of happiness that wafted up from the crowd as they cheered. I forced a genuine smile as Gus dipped his new bride and her giddy gaze found mine from across the room. She looked beautiful today. Dianna would be proud of her. Of them both. Lottie prolonged the engagement for as long as she could. She said she wasn't ready, but we all knew why. The same reason I look twice at every beautiful woman with curls as black as night.

We all thought you'd come back.

These last four years were almost as hard as a hundred aboard The Black Soul. But I know now...she's never coming. I'll admit, a part of me expected her to return. After she fled to the future to save her mother, I truly thought Dianna would come back to us. To me. I know her heart belongs to Henry, but mine belongs to her. Whether she wants it or not. And, try as I might, there's nothing I can do to change that.

"I've never seen anyone look so miserable at a party," spoke a voice as someone approached from behind and sidled up to me. Roselyn. Her silky black hair draped down across her fancy golden corset. "Care to dance?"

I sighed and downed the rest of the ale in my mug. "No."

She crossed her arms and stood in the silence that wrapped around me. After a few moments, she tried again.

"Are you looking forward to the long journey tomorrow?"

I guffawed and tipped my chin toward the crowd. "Stuck on The Queen with this lot for the next three months? Not really. But they're my crew... *she* insisted on it. I go where they go. And Lottie says we can have a life there."

Roselyn didn't dare comment on who *she* was, knowing very well it pained me to talk about it. She inhaled through her nose, long and hard, and peered through the dancing fools where the newlyweds twirled together.

"Why don't you wait until after the baby is here? Stay a while longer."

"Lottie doesn't want to be sailing with a newborn," I told her. "It's best we go now, or we'll be stuck here for another four years."

Truthfully, some part of me, deep down inside, longed to be some place she's been. Just the thought of touching foot on the same land that Dianna might very well be pacing somewhere in another time. It made me feel closer to her. As ridiculous as the idea may be.

The song ended and the band set their instruments down for a break. Lottie kissed Gus on the cheek and bounded across the room toward me. I heard Roselyn moan at my side, and I turned to find her rolling her eyes.

"That's my cue to leave," she said and turned her back to an approaching Lottie. Her slender brown fingers caressed my shoulder as she leaned into my ear. "I'll see you tonight, then? Before you leave?"

Dianna would probably kill me for sleeping with Roselyn. But I'm a weak man with a weaker heart, and I long for human connection. Or maybe it helps distract me from thoughts of her, if only for a night. I wiped the ale from my beard and closed my eyes as I fought off a sigh.

"Of course, as always."

I listened to her footsteps fade away behind my back as Lottie came to a stop in front of me. Her yellow hair left loose around her shoulders made her look like a little doll, with cheeks flushed from dancing. She smiled and huffed to catch her breath.

"Want to dance?" she asked jokingly, knowing I'd say no.

I grabbed an empty chair and hauled it over. "Sit," I told her. "You're exhausted."

"It's my wedding day," she replied. "Aren't I supposed to be?"

I grumbled a response.

Lottie took a seat and wrangled her hair into some sort of heap atop her head. "What did Roselyn want?"

"Just came to make sure I was having fun."

"What a shame she had to find you like this then," Lottie joked and peered up at me with a cheeky grin.

"I'm enjoying myself," I defended. "It's nice to see you guys finally go through with it."

She rubbed her modest bump and smiled. "Yeah, well, time was starting to run out. Wouldn't want this one born a bastard now, would we?" When I didn't respond, she added. "Will you miss her?"

A rush of adrenaline rushed through my veins as a small flicker in my mind assumed she meant

Dianna. I relaxed and leaned against the wall. "Roselyn? Sure. A little. I mean, she's been good to us."

"Only because she feels guilty for what she did," Lottie argued. "Roselyn Wallace is no friend of ours. Wretched creature for what she allowed happen right here in her own home."

"She threw you this wedding, didn't she? Besides, before, she wasn't left with much of a choice," I defended. "Roselyn's tried her best to make up for it. She's just... on the outside. Like me."

Lottie sat up straight and turned to face me. "Ben, you're not on the outside. You're one of us. Dianna left The Queen to *us*. We're a crew. We're a *family*."

I cringed at the sound of her name spoken out loud. They were always so careful not to say it around me. In the beginning, during those first few months after she left, I was torn apart inside. I acted out of anger on most days. She was ripped away before I got the chance to show her how much I appreciated this gift she gave me. Before we had a chance to... I don't know. Just... a chance for *anything*.

Lottie stood up and pat me on the back. "Look, I miss them, too. But it's been years, Ben. You have to live this life you've been given. Everything will be better once we get to Newfoundland. A fresh start. I promise."

I nodded and managed a weak smile. She kissed my cheek and made her way back through the crowd as the music began playing again, filling the large area with noise. I swiped a full bottle of rum from one of the tables and bounded for the front door. Away from everyone, from all the blaring sounds that assaulted my ears. It made it hard to think straight.

But as I strut across the front lawn of The Siren's Call, heading for town, something Lottie said stuck in my mind. She misses them. I took a swig of rum as my boots crunched the dry gravel of the path that led away from the house. Well, I don't miss *them*.

No, there's only one person I long for in this world and it's *you*.

Dianna.

***

You'd think that after four years I'd be able to stop thinking about her. But I'd be lying if I said I could. Not a day has gone by where I don't have the image of her face flash across my mind. It's some kind of torture. And yet... most days I find myself searching. For a sign. For something...*anything* that reminds me of her.

Dianna...

I muttered your name in my mind as I rolled over and placed a gentle kiss on the naked back of the woman lying next to me. Meredith, a lady of the evening. Excellent company and a welcome distraction I often took comfort in. Aside from the nights I spent in Roselyn's bed.

Her fiery red hair blazed against the grey linens as she slept. I swung my legs over the side of the bed and searched for my trousers. The bed jostled from behind as she stirred from sleep and I suddenly felt her warm body pressed against my back. Her fingers raked through my hair, but I continued to shove a foot inside my trousers.

"You pirates and your gorgeous wild hair," Meredith spoke against the side of my face. "Why the hurry to leave?"

"I got a date with a lady," I replied.

Her lips caressed my ear. "I'm a lady."

"Trust me," I guffawed. "You're nothing like this woman."

She huffed and then leaned against the headboard as I stood. "And why's that? Do not assume I can't be a lady just because I'm a whore, Benjamin." Her arms crossed tightly over her naked chest as she shrugged. "What's this woman got that I don't, anyway?"

With a grin, I leaned across the bed and placed a slow, gentle kiss along her jaw before giving her a wink. "Well, for starters, you're human."

***

I could hear the gentle crashing of waves against wet stone as I made my way across the field just down from The Siren's Call. Where I went every night. I don't know what made me come back here, time and time again. But, if the crew were on land, that's where I'd be. And sometimes even where I'd wake up.

I set my half bottle of rum down on the ground before removing my boots and stopped for a quick moment to roll up the legs of my pants to the knee. It felt good to have the damp, cold grass on the skin of my feet. I stepped across to a low, flat rock and sat down. Dangling my feet over the side and dipped them in the crisp ocean water.

With a sigh, I took a long swig of rum and gazed out over the surface; gentle waves lopping about. The silver light of the moon penetrating the obsidian waters. I couldn't help but wonder...

Were you looking at the sea at that very moment?

Suddenly, a break in the water revealed something emerging. A face. One I'd come to know so well. She smiled; a toothy grin that formed as she shifted from her clear liquid state to a more solid form. The siren's hair gleamed in the moonlight just as her skin did, with an eerie glow.

"You are thinking about her again, aren't you?" she asked me in a layered musical voice.

I took comfort in the way the sound seemed to come from all around, from the very ocean itself, enveloping me in a conflicting embrace. The ocean was my home. I knew it better than any place on land. Especially now, in this foreign future. I've missed so much. And still...

Confliction.

I'd spent so many decades trapped aboard The Black Soul with my brother that the ocean became a prison. A dark layer stacked on top of a short life's worth of good memories. Being near the water, it brings me solitude. And yet, I will never forget the darkness.

I'm thinking of you again.

I wonder what she's doing. If she misses it at all; the adventure, The Queen, her friends. Me. Such a quick flame we created in one another's lives. But no one has ever left such a mark on me before. Dianna saved my soul. She ended the curse and gave me a second chance at life. But now she'll never see me live it and I'll never be able to repay her for what she's given me.

"Yeah," I finally replied, willing myself to remain in the present. I scooped up a handful of pebbles and began mindlessly tossing them in the water. "I can't help it."

The siren swam closer to me. I loved it when she got close. When I could see the details of her magnificent existence a little better. Because it really was miraculous. Beautiful, even. Skin like the silvery underside of a trout. Hair made of kelp, dark and red.

Her long fingers gripped the edge of the rock next to my leg as two massive black eyes beamed up at me. "Why is it so hard?"

I shrugged and took another swig. "It's been too long," I said. "People have changed over a hundred years. I can't... I can't seem to connect. It feels as though I'm always looking in from the outside."

"But you did not feel this way with Dianna," the siren stated, already knowing the answer. I just nodded in response. "What of your friends aboard The Queen?"

I let out a puff of air and looked across the gleaming water. I thought about the crew; silent Gus. Lottie and her growing belly as she carries his child. It reminds me of Dianna. They lead the ship well enough and try their hardest to make me feel at home. And Finn... it's hard not to like the Scot. I've enjoyed the adventures I've shared with them but, still, I catch their side glances and walk in on their whispers. They know I love her and they're all careful not to speak her name too much in my presence. I'm not able to settle.

"They're not my friends. I have no friends."

She moved closer; the gentle water lapped against the rock by my legs. I could smell the sea radiating from her scaly skin. "I am your friend, Benjamin Cook."

"Is that so?" I laughed. "I suppose you are. We speak just about every night." Another swig. "But, even after all these years, you've yet to tell me your name."

"I am a siren -"

"No, no," I cut her off and she gave me a puzzled look. "Your *real* name. You must have one, don't you?"

She stared at me thoughtfully for a few moments before blinking and then her mouth curved up at the sides. "I am a siren of the sea. Part Fae. It is unwise to reveal a given name in my world. It would give power over me to those whose mouths possess it."

"Don't you trust me?" I asked her, only half-serious. I wouldn't trust me either. A once cursed pirate who helped steal the heart right from her sister's chest. I often wondered why the siren came to me each night. Why she spent so much time in my presence. Not that I wasn't grateful. I felt more connected to this creature of the sea than any human on land.

Still, she seemed to ponder the thought. The idea of trusting me.

"What would you give me in return?" she asked.

"What? Like a gift?"

"More of an... *exchange*," the siren replied almost deviously. "A secret for a secret. Tell me what your heart most desires and I'll give you my name, Benjamin Cook."

I heaved a heavy sigh and laid back on the ground behind me, legs still dangling in the cold ocean water. I stared up at the pure white moon above and pretended to think about what my heart wanted, but I was a fool to even try. I already knew the answer before my mind could even dream up the words.

You.

"I dream that I could see Dianna, you know?" I confessed. "Just one more time. Tell her I miss her. To really get the chance to thank her for what she did for me. It all feels so unfinished. She was taken away too soon. Too fast. Before I got the chance." I sat up then with a long guffaw. "Wishes. God damn wishes. Not everyone has a magical pearl bracelet, I suppose."

The siren dipped her hand back into the water and plucked a tiny object from it before outstretching her arm to reveal a black pearl pinched between her fingers.

"You mean, such as this?" she quipped.

It couldn't possibly be real. This was an illusion, something she'd shown me many times before. For fun. The siren fascinated me with everything she did, especially magic.

"What would you wish for if you only had one?" Her lips curled with every word.

I swiped the pearl from her grasp and chuckled as I rolled it around in my fingers. "I wish Dianna would come back. With or without Henry, it wouldn't matter."

The siren's eyes narrowed. "Done."

"Wait! Where are you going?" I asked the creature as she ducked down under the water. "Tell me your name!"

She popped her head back up and smiled at me. "A secret for a secret. Very well. My name is Seneca Saye, Benjamin Cook." Her expression cocked to the side. "I'll return soon. I must pay a visit to someone who -" her smile twisted into a coy grin, "owes me a favor."

CHAPTER TWO

It's hard to think about the future when your head is stuck in the past. A future for myself and Henry, for our two beautiful children. But I can't. It takes all I have just to hold myself together each day. For them. For Arthur and Audrey.

And for Henry.

I dragged him through the sands of time to a world he knew nothing of. And he followed me blindly with his heart in tow, not caring about what awaited him on the other side. He's adjusted well enough. But, still, I carry that guilt.

After four long years, you'd think I could let it go. Not a single day has gone by that I haven't thought of our friends we left behind. What became of them? Are they all alright? Henry and I spent months searching history books and records for any sign of our crew. But we found nothing. As if they never even existed.

It's difficult to find resolute within myself for the things that happened. During those first few years, I had the pregnancy and the birth of our children to distract me. But it didn't take long for my thoughts and worries to wander to the past.

Especially after the siren reared its head.

The sea creature appeared to me three months ago, demanding I uphold my end of some fickle bargain I'd blindly made... and forgotten about. Back when we were all stranded on Shellbed Isle after retrieving Peter Easton's lost treasure. But a lot had happened since then. I'd found out just how much those wretched creatures have meddled in the lives of Cobham women. For hundreds of years. I felt no obligation to keep my promise to the beast.

Still, she kept coming.

Twice more. The siren appeared to me by the water, insisting that I keep my promise of a single favor. When my curiosity finally caved and I gave her an inch, I asked what she wanted of me. I wasn't prepared for what the creature said. Yet, part of me expected the words before she spoke them.

She wanted me to return to the past.

Her voice rang in my memory as I stood and stared out the picture window that looked over the ocean by my house. The sun was high in the sky and cast a warm glow over the crystal waters. I gripped a rolled-up blanket and a basket of food in my hands as I stood there thoughtfully, swaying gently to the waves of thoughts in my head.

What if the siren appears again? When I'm by the water with Henry. Would he be tempted to go back? He's found comfort in the little life we've built here in this quiet corner of the earth. But he's yet to fully adjust to the modern world. Things like cars and technology unease him. I took him to St. John's once to do some sightseeing and catch a movie. He just about lost his mind in the theater.

If he knew there was a way back, would he take it?

After the children were born, we'd made a promise to one another. No searching. No going back. And definitely, no telling the kids that time travel was real. We threw everything in a trunk and locked it tightly before burying it deep in the woods. But that was before. When we were high on the thrill of time travelling and saving everyone from my evil sister. Now that the dust has settled, I often wondered if he longed for the sea. For the past.

For the life of a pirate.

A hand touched the small of my back and I gasped as the sensation ripped me from the dark daydream. "What are you thinking about?" Henry asked quietly against my ear, sending a shiver down my spine.

His fingers trailed up my back and gripped my ponytail, tugging ever so gently, but enough to tip my head back. His warm mouth touched the crook of my neck and I smiled.

"Just wondering if it's too cold to take the kids down to the beach," I replied and let myself melt into his embrace as he held me from behind.

The blonde scruff on his face tickled my skin as he continued to leave tiny kisses along the side of my throat. "They'll be fine," he assured me and then let out a single, raspy chuckle. "They're the offspring of two ruthless pirates."

I set the blanket and basket of food down on the table before I spun around in his arms. "Only one of us was ever a ruthless pirate."

Henry arched an eyebrow and those dark eyes glistened in the sunlight that poured in through the window. Like embers in a fire. He chuckled, low and raspy.

"You're right. I was a simple man, swayed by your merciless ways and harlot looks. The ruthless pirate queen."

I laughed and playfully slapped his chest, but it only made him hold me tighter. One arm wrapped around my waist, his other held my face, fingers twisted in the loose curls that had escaped the elastic band that failed to hold it all in place. His lips came to mine in a hard, warm press and all my worries melted away.

No matter the darkness in my life, Henry was always there to chase it back. I could feel his love like a tangible thing, something real, something never wavering. I suddenly felt like a fool for worrying he'd ever leave me for a second chance at a life of piracy. He belonged here with me, and I with him. Our foreheads pressed together as we stood in the dining room, locked in one another's embrace.

The alarming sound of little footsteps bombarding down the stairs stole my attention and the kids came stampeding through the kitchen shouting, "Beach!". They whipped between Henry and me, severing the intimate moment, and threw the patio door open before barrelling down the backyard toward the water.

Henry laughed as he grabbed the basket of food and tucked the blanket under an arm. He offered his free hand. "Shall we?"

With a heart full of love for the little family we created here, I took his hand and walked together to the ocean.

***

I laid back on the quilted blanket as the setting sun warmed the ocean surface with colors of orange and purple, my journal opened by my side. I wrote in it as Henry nursed the fire he built and readied the hot dogs for roasting. I loved evenings like this. Arthur and Audrey were squat in the sand, building castles and digging holes for the incoming tide to flood. Life was good.

Most of the time.

I don't know why I write in this journal Lottie once gave me. But I do. At first, it was a way for me to feel connected to my friends in the past, even though I knew they'd never read the words on the pages. Still, I documented every major milestone, every thought, memory, or feeling. Its papers now worn and browned from the years of use, their numbers running out as I neared the end.

I glanced up with a smile as the kids squealed with delight at the chilly water that rushed in. But a second look froze me in place. My heart stopped as the blood in my veins seared with a painful dose of panic.

Audrey was gone.

"Arthur, where's your sister?" I asked as I leaped to my feet. My head whipped around in alarm. "*Arthur!*"

Henry was at my side. "What's wrong?"

"Audrey's gone," I quickly replied and took three long strides toward my son. He was visibly shaken, and I knelt down to take him in my arms. "It's okay, baby. Where did Audrey go?"

"I don't know, Mommy," his sweet little voice said sadly. Snot dripped from his nose as his eyes filled with tears. "S-she gotted swallowed up."

My eyes widened and Henry tensed as he turned and peered out over the water.

"What do you mean she got swallowed up, baby?" I pressed gently, trying my best to hide the stone-cold fear that was taking over my body.

His blonde little head slowly turned, and he pointed toward the sea. I heard Henry inhale a sharp breath of air before running and diving into the water. I scooped Arthur up in my arms and held him tight to my chest as I began frantically pacing the shoreline, my eyes scanning every nook and cranny. Every jagged rock. Every tide pool.

But my little girl was nowhere to be found.

I stood on a slick rock as the wind whipped through my hair and a realization struck me with a painful truth. Tears streamed from my eyes and my lips trembled as I choked out a single whisper.

"No..."

My shaking arms gripped Arthur firmly as his head nestled into the crook of my neck, a place he often took comfort when he was scared.

"No!" I screamed at the water. "Bring her back! *Please*!"

The cold waves beat against the stone on which I stood, gently flooding over its surface. I felt helpless. I felt like plunging into the ocean and giving myself in exchange for my daughter. Do what you will with me but give her back.

"Mommy?" said a musical little voice from behind me.

I spun around and my heart sprang to life at the sight of Audrey standing on the rock as if she'd always been there. I knelt down and grabbed her with one arm, the other still holding her brother, and squeezed as tears of relief poured down my face.

"Oh my God, baby," I cried and kissed her soaking wet face. "Where have you been?"

She leaned away and stared up at me in a daze. Her long blonde hair, caked with sand and saltwater, clung to her cherub face. She didn't answer me.

"Audrey," I said and gave her a little shake. "Are you alright?"

She blinked a few times and then her eyes finally focused on me, as if seeing me for the first time. Her lips, greyed and purple, turned up in a smile. "Mommy, why are you crying?"

"We couldn't find you," I told her. "I was worried."

"I..." she glanced around, taking in her surroundings. "I was right here."

Henry came running over, splashing in the water with every giant step he took, his arm swinging as he fought to get to us as fast as he could. He grabbed Audrey and took her in his arms, kissed her head. We exchanged a concerned look but said nothing in front of the kids. They were already too shaken up. He knew something was wrong, and I feared my only worry for the last three months was forcing its way out. I'd have to tell him about the siren.

"Let's get you two back to the house and dried off before bed, hey?" he said to them. He peered up at me, still standing on the rock, and held out his free arm. "Here, let me take him."

Slowly, I nodded and let Henry peel Arthur from my side. He held them both with ease and walked out of the water, toward our home. My emotions were all over the place, holding me a prisoner in my own body, nailed down by fear. Could the siren have been behind this? Could it truly go to such an unbelievable length to get my attention?

Before I stepped off the long rock that jutted out of the shoreline, something pressed against my barefoot. A tiny pebble lapped at my toe as the wet surface sloshed about. I bent down and picked it up, rolling it between my fingers as I brought it to my face. A new sense of fear washed over me as I realized it wasn't a stone at all. It was a pearl. A message—no—a warning.

The siren was done being patient.

The pearl, such a tiny thing, meant so much more than anyone could ever imagine. *Make a wish and come back to the past …*

… or I take your children.

CHAPTER THREE

The sun shined in through the large window of my bedroom and warmed my face from an odd angle. My tired eyes pried open and blinked away the sleepy film that covered them, a low moan escaping my chest as I let out a yawn. I stretched my arm out for Henry but found nothing more than a cold heap of blankets on his side of the bed. What time was it? With a grumble, I rolled over and checked my phone. Nearly noon.

I peeled the sheets off my bone-weary body and swung my legs over the side as I gripped the edges of the mattress to heave a sigh. This week had wreaked havoc on my nerves and the physical toll that stress was putting on my body was beginning to catch up with me. Every day, I obsessed over the siren's warning. The pearl that sat in the drawer of my bedside table; carefully tucked away in a small locked box. Why did the creature want me to come back to the past so badly? My mind had long spiraled into a swarm of possibilities and I couldn't break free of the thoughts.

Were our friends in trouble?

Did someone die?

Has Benjamin settled into his new life, free of the curse?

I often wondered about him. The man who stumbled into my life with such a force, with such a heart. He wore it on his sleeve, and it made being his friend easy. I know he loved me, but I also know he respected our friendship. I helped to break the curse that held him a prisoner aboard The Black Soul for over a hundred years, but I sometimes worried that he never adjusted to life in the eighteenth century after we left. Did he feel out of place, like Henry often did here in this time?

I stood and plucked my robe from the hook on the back of our bedroom door before wandering out to the hall. Strange. The house was completely silent, aside from the sounds of the push and pull of waves just outside.

I walked downstairs as a heavy aroma of freshly brewed coffee greeted my nose and I smiled. Henry must have made it before taking the kids outside. I poured myself a cup and grinned as I recalled those first moments of Henry's life here in the future.

How he cooked food and boiled water over the wood stove for months before feeling comfortable enough to use the gas stovetop.

Everything he's done to build a life for us here has been for me and the kids. How could I ever think, even for a second, that he would leave me for the chance to resume his old life? The man I pulled from the past was nothing less than eager to leave that all behind. I'd do well to remember that.

The unnatural silence that filled the house made me uneasy. I was so used to the vibrant sounds of the kids bouncing off the walls from the moment the sun comes up. It felt strange to stand in the kitchen, surrounded by the stark quiet. Henry must have taken them for a bike ride down the road to mom's house. But when I opened the front door and found their little bicycles, haphazardly thrown on the lawn as they usually are, I realized I was wrong.

I walked back through the house with my warm coffee mug in hand, sipping carefully as I strolled toward the large picture window that overlooked our beachy backyard, expecting to find them playing on the swing set Henry built for them. But the empty swings blew in the afternoon breeze that came in off the ocean. My eyes scanned along the sandy line that met the long grass of our yard and my heart squeezed in my chest. All the blood rushed to my tightened chest and my fingers went numb. *No, he can't.* The coffee cup slipped from my hands and crashed to the floor with a sound that screeched against the walls with a painful echo.

Henry was lifting the kids in the boat.

"No," I frantically whispered and ran for the patio door.

I ripped it open and bolted down across the lawn, my bare feet catching on all the jagged rocks that hid beneath the long green blades. But it didn't phase me.

"Henry!" I screamed. "Henry, stop!"

His head popped up, a look of fright and confusion on his face as I finally approached the boat and gripped its edges. I took a second to catch my breath.

"Dianna," he said with concern. "What's wrong?"

"You can't take them," I said, exasperated.

"What? I'm just -"

"*I said you can't take them*!" I snapped. Tears swelled in my eyes. Desperation had taken hold of me and my fears were rearing their ugly heads. "N-not on the water. Please." I begged him with my eyes as his searched for some answers within mine. "I can't handle it... not after last week."

Arthur tugged at my sleeve. "Mommy, I want to go in the boat!"

I plastered on a smile and leaned down to his sweet little face. "I know, baby, but not today. Some other time, I promise." I scooped him up, life jacket and all, and lifted him from the boat before doing the same with his sister. "Why don't you guys ride your bikes?"

"I don't wanna ride bike," Arthur whined. "I want to go in the boat with Daddy."

"I made sure they were wearing life coats, Dianna," Henry assured me. A look of hurt flashed across his face as his glistening black eyes continued to search my frantic stare. "They're safe with me, I swear."

I shook my head. "I know. I just... I can't..."

My throat tightened at I thought of the siren taking my children and I struggled to contain myself. I wrapped my arms tightly across my chest. Henry reached out and grasped my arm comfortingly as he lowered his voice to a soothing tone.

"Alright." He stepped closer and rubbed his hand over the cotton sleeve of my robe. "It's okay. I'll take them fishing down by the creek where it's safer. There are only a few inches of water there and I won't take my eyes off them."

I inhaled a blubbery breath of air and nodded as my shaking hand wiped at the wetness streaming down my cheeks. Relief struck me hard. Not because Henry promised to watch them by the creek, but because I knew it was nowhere near the ocean. The siren was a creature of the sea and had no bearing on fresh land water.

His finger slipped under my chin and tipped my head up to look at him. He wiped at the tears that pooled over my lips and placed a gentle kiss there. When he pulled away and I immediately felt myself calming. Henry had that effect on me. My anchor in the madness of the world.

"Are you alright?"

"I'm fine," I insisted with a shrug. A poor attempt to brush off my nerves. "Just shaken up after last week, you know?"

"Why don't you head back to the house and relax?" he replied and turned to grab the fishing rods from the boat. He spun around with a playful grin. "I'll bring home supper."

I laughed, surprised by how good it felt. "Okay. You guys have fun."

Henry kissed me once more before running off after the kids who were playing happily on their swing set, my behaviour already long forgotten. Their cherubic faces pinched with laughter as Henry ran up and gave them each a big push, sending them soaring on their swings. The sounds of their innocent squeals of delight warmed my heart and forced my breathing to calm.

I stood there on the sand and watched as Arthur and Audrey hopped down and followed Henry like two little ducklings. The three of them disappeared around the front of the house, toward the safety of the treeline on the other side of the road, away from the ocean and all the dangers that awaited them. I'd saved them this time, but how long could I continue with this? How long could I prevent my family from going to the ocean? And worse...

How long until the siren lost her patience altogether?

***

I closed the storybook in my lap and stood from the rocking chair that sat in the corner of the kid's room. My old bedroom. Henry and I divided the space with two twin beds for Arthur and Audrey to share. Their sleeping faces were soft and pink. They slept soundly as I bent down to tuck them in and kiss those sweet little foreheads. They were my world. Two tiny creatures nestled in their beds; a stuffed animal gripped tightly in each of their arms. I would do anything for them. If only they knew the adventures I had while they were safe in my belly. I sometimes wondered if I would ever tell them. One day.

As I was nearing the door, Audrey spoke. Her musical voice croaky and tired.

"Why are you scared of the water, Mommy?"

I spun around slowly and stepped softly back to her bed. "What do you mean, sweetie?"

"You don't like the ocean anymore?"

I sighed. "No, I do, baby. Mommy loves the ocean. But sometimes I get scared that you and your brother might get hurt."

She reached under her blanket and surprisingly pulled out a bracelet. Handmade by her; I could see that in the miss-matched pattern of colored beads. A single shell stuffed in the middle.

"I made this for you," she whispered.

My cheeks warmed with love as she slipped it over my hand and the elastic snapped in place.

"Thank you," I told her. "It's beautiful."

"It will protect you," she said matter-of-factly.

I feigned surprise. "Oh, well, in that case, we should make one for you, too."

Audrey yawned and pulled her blanket up tight around her face as her eyelids fluttered under the weight of sleep. "That's okay. The ocean promised not to hurt me..."

My eyes widened and my head whipped around to stare accusingly out the window that looked over the ocean. Could the siren have spoken to my daughter when she plucked her from the beach that day?

"What else did the ocean say?" I asked her, but she was already asleep.

With a nervous sigh, I kissed her forehead and closed the door behind me before strolling across the hall and down to where Henry waited in the kitchen. I stopped at the foot of the stairs and watched as he chopped apple slices and poured two cups of tea. Our nighttime ritual.

"Kids asleep?" he asked as he stirred in some honey. All the hard muscles of his wide shoulders and long arms flexed beneath his t-shirt with every slight move. A lock of blonde hair fell from the elastic that loosely tied it all back. What little he still kept, anyway.

"Both out like a light." I leaned against the archway, watching him work.

He peered up at me, the corner of his mouth curving. "Are you going to just stand there, or would you care to join me for some tea by the fire?"

I grinned and raised my brow mockingly. "I'm just enjoying the view."

Henry grabbed a steaming mug in each hand and sauntered over to me. I reached for one of the cups, but he held it away and playfully leaned in toward my face. I laughed and kissed his mouth, melting into the way his warm lips took mine. Such a simple, intimate thing. But Henry had a way of making it feel like every kiss was our first. As if I were the only woman in the world. The way time seemed to slow around us, how his soft mouth pressed against mine with purpose. With meaning.

I moaned with quiet delight as his lips lingered around mine and he opened his eyes. I grabbed the collar of his shirt and gave a little tug. "Don't ever let a day go by without kissing me. Alright?"

Het let me take one of the mugs. "That's a tall order."

I shoved at his shoulder. "Promise?"

"Whatever milady wants." He gave me another quick peck before turning back to the kitchen island where he was preparing the tea. "You seem in better spirits now. Everything alight?"

"Yeah, I just..." I struggled to find the right words to say. "I'm anxious about the water after Audrey disappeared last week."

His finger traced the rim of the cup he held. His gaze thoughtfully falling to the floor. "You know, they would have been okay. With me. I would have made sure they were safe."

My heart sank and I took two quick steps toward him. "Oh, Henry, no. It's not like that. There's no one I trust more than you. With *anything*. I was just nervous, is all. After I lost my mom to the sea for so many years... I just couldn't bear it if it happened to the kids."

He was silent for a moment as he took in my words.

"Is that all?" he finally asked.

The hairs on my arms stood on end and my eyes widened. "What do you mean?"

"You've not been yourself for a few weeks now," he told me. "I pay attention to every breath you take, Dianna. Did you not think I would notice how you get lost in your own mind? How distracted you've been? Your shortness with the kids?"

My mouth gaped open as my brain raced for answers. For anything to give him that could explain my behavior. I gripped the warm cup of tea between two hands and turned my head to peer out the window.

"I love living by the sea," I told him and chewed at my lip. "But it reminds me of them every day."

I didn't need to say much more than that. Henry knew who I meant. Our friends. Our crew. The family that we left back in the past.

"Dianna..." he said, almost a whisper. He wanted me to talk, to tell him what was going on in my mind. But Henry knew me better than most. He knew I wasn't ready to talk about it.

I craned my neck and looked pointedly in his dark eyes. "Do you think about them? About the life we left behind?"

He set his cup down and crossed his arms. "Of course. I mean, not all the time. But there are moments when something reminds me of them." He guffawed. "Especially when the kids eat. Reminds me much of Finn. Whenever I remove a knife from the wooden block, I think of Lottie."

"Do you think they're still alive?"

He heaved a deep, raspy sigh and joined me in gazing out the window to the midnight blue ocean.

"We searched every history book, every record we could find," he reminded me. "There was nothing. As if they never even existed in the first place."

I rubbed at my tired face. Henry's hand reached over and caressed my back.

"But I have every faith that they are indeed alive," he added and then let out a slight chuckle. "They're all far too stubborn to die."

I stood and sipped my tea. The warmth comforted me as it made its way down through my body and I held the rim to my nose to inhale the sweet aroma.

"Why are you thinking of them?" Henry asked. "Do you miss the dirty grimy life aboard a pirate ship?"

I laughed and set my cup down on the table under the window. I threw my arms around his neck and I gazed into those gorgeous black eyes.

"The only thing I miss is your lips when they're not on me."

Henry's gaze intensified as his brow lowered and a deep hum erupted from his chest. "Then let's fix that, shall we?"

His massive frame loomed over me as he pulled me closer and we swayed slowly in unison. Henry had a way of making me feel small and safe in his arms, yet never let me down from the pedestal he put me on. I was his world and he was mine; together with our children, we were a happy family. Complete and whole. The life we've built was a warm and comfortable one and I never wanted any of that to change. Henry's happiness was evident in almost everything he did. I felt like a fool for even questioning it.

The blonde scruff of his face trailed along my jaw and nestled in my ear. His breath tickled my skin and my body responded with a rush of hot goosebumps. I pressed my frame tight to his and Henry's strong arm wrapped around my waist, holding me desperately. He brushed the hair from my face as he held my cheek and kissed my lips. One of those scorching, all-encompassing kisses that sent my insides reeling. I was mush in his capable arms.

In a split second, Henry slid both hands under my bottom and hoisted me up on the kitchen island. I opened my legs and welcomed him before wrapping them tightly around his torso. My head tossed back as my body arched toward his mouth that slowly trailed down the tender skin of my neck. My chest between my bosom. His long fingers crept up under the hem of my nightie beneath the cotton robe I wore, and a moan escaped my lips.

I could feel Henry's mouth morph into a wide grin at the sounds he elicited from my body and his head dipped between my legs, his lips leaving tender stamps along my inner thigh. The world around me faded away as I gave myself over to him and thoughts of sirens and time travel fled my mind. For now.

Tomorrow was another day.

CHAPTER FOUR

I closed the heavy metal door to the bakery and waved goodbye to the last customer; a local man and father. He was one of many parents who came in today to get baked goods and a free cookie for his daughter. Free Cookie Sundays were something Mom insisted stayed alive when we took over the bakery from my cousin. My contribution was a giant pot of homemade soup, a different kind every week. The last four years had been good to us. Cobham Bakery and Café has become more than just a tourist stop. We're the most popular place to grab fresh baked goods and a warm homemade meal on the West Coast and it's allowed us to stay open all year round.

Just another piece of the perfect little life we've created here in this time.

"Everyone loved your soup today," Mom said from behind the counter. I turned to find her already elbow-deep in the dishes from the day, loading them into the industrial dishwasher.

"And everyone devoured your baked goods as usual," I replied, checking the empty shelves we had out front.

Only one loaf of bread remained. I grabbed it and stared out the window. The long dirt road that led to the bakery disappeared in the distance and seemed to point to the horizon. The ocean, far in the background, silently crashed against the rocky shore. It was hypnotizing. The way it moved with such a beautiful and raw force. It was no wonder the sea had a hold on the threads of time. The ocean was like a titan, a mythical being that existed outside the realm of comprehension. Always changing, never yielding.

"So, when are you going to tell me what's been bothering you?" Mom piped up and broke through the daze I fell into.

"What?" I said and turned to her.

She didn't bother to look at me as she expertly wiped down all the surfaces and equipment behind the counter. "Baby, I'm your mother. I know when something's wrong simply by the way your breathing changes."

I let out a long huff of air. Henry said something akin to that. Was I that obvious, or did they truly know me that well? "Why did Martha pull you back to the past?"

Mom came to a halt and stared across the bakery at me. "Why do you ask?"

I shrugged and walked toward the counter between us. "I don't know. No reason, I guess. I've just been thinking about our friends in the past lately. Wondering about them. So much time has gone by, and I worry I'll forget little details. So, I've been asking myself a lot of questions." I paused and held her worried gaze. "Like the details surrounding you. You once told me that the witch, she pulled you back to the past when I was a kid. But you never told me why."

She tossed the rag down and removed her apron before waltzing around the countertop where she leaned back against it and crossed her arms.

"It wasn't Martha directly," she told me. My brow pinched together in confusion. "The sirens did. It didn't take me long to discover that Martha had made some sort of deal with the creatures to bring me back. The Celtic witches are firm believers in the sanctity of time. It should be intact, and they're strictly against time travel. In fact, they call themselves the keepers of time in some countries." She stopped to heave a sigh; the words clearly heavy on her. This wasn't something Mom often spoke about. "Martha was like a mother to me, her coven practically raised me. When she realized what I'd done, she was furious."

I let her words pass through me, my mind

carefully working through it all. "So, how did you come here to begin with? Before you met Dad."

Mom grinned and shook her finger at me as she walked over to the coat rack and grabbed her jacket. "That's a story for another time."

"Mom -"

"I'm not ready to share that part of my life, Dianna," she asserted with wide eyes. "It holds no bearing on the life I live now. I was young and foolish."

I stared at my mother, the enigma. Her long black curls now streaked with grey, her heart-shaped face pinched in places from years of laughing and frowning. I was almost an exact copy of her, and I found myself pondering if I'd be in this same position one day, refusing to tell my children about the adventurous life I lived. Henry and I swore we'd keep our past in the past, never tell the kids about time travel or pirates. Everything that came from that life was buried deep in the woods. But now I wondered... was that the right thing to do?

I didn't have a response for her but nodded as she slipped on her jacket and walked over to me. She placed a comforting hand on my shoulder and smiled. "Make peace with that, baby. I have. My life is wonderful and I'm grateful for each day forward."

"I know, Mom," I replied. "I am, too. Henry and the kids..." I took a deep breath, "they're everything to me."

We stepped outside and Mom locked the door

behind her as I waited. The warm afternoon sun beamed down and fought through the chilly mist in the air. The final lingering signs of Spring. I was so looking forward to the summer.

"Funny he didn't bring them in for their free cookie today," she said as we walked toward our cars. "He must have taken them fishing."

My heart stopped. "What?"

Mom looked over her shoulder as she unlocked her car door. "Henry. Doesn't he usually take the kids fishing on Sundays?"

My eyes bulged as my mind refused to relent to the fear that suddenly struck me down. "*No...*"

Stiff from the frigid anxiety that threatened to take over my body, I painfully flew into a fight-or-flight mode and bound for my car. Mom was speaking to me, but her words banged against my mind in quiet muffles. My shaking hands fumbled with the keys, but I shoved them in the slot and turned over the engine of my Jeep. It roared to life and I sped off down the dirt road, tearing up the rocks and billows of dust in my wake.

I knew it was only a few minute's drive home, but it felt like forever before I pulled up out front. My lungs, constricted by dread, refused to fully inflate and I began to enter a full-on panic attack as I leaped from the car and ran around to the back of the house. I stopped for a quick moment, scanning frantically over the shoreline. The high afternoon sun blinding me. I raised a hand to protect my eyes and found nothing on the water. Not a speck. But something was on the beach. An upturned boat next to a cracked oar and a lifeless body.

"Henry!" I screamed and clumsily ran down the expanse of grass behind our home, straight for the beach where my husband lay on his stomach. I fell to his side and flipped him over. His skin pale, lips greyed, and no sign of breathing.

"Damn it, Henry!" I screamed again and began chest compressions. Tears flowed from down my cheeks as I used all my might to pump life back into the man I loved. And not for the first time. "Come on," I spoke to him, "breath!"

Finally, his body tightened and convulsed, and he rolled to his side to spew the water from his lungs. I reeled back and put my tired weight on my heels as I fought to catch my breath.

"Dianna?" Henry said hoarsely, confusion evident in his tone. He glanced around and his eyes bulged.

"Where are the kids?" I asked him. He didn't answer, he just kept searching the sand around us in disbelief. I grabbed his shoulders and shook. "Henry! Where are our children?"

He ran a hand tightly through his disheveled wet hair. "I-I don't... they were just..."

"No." Tears began to roll harder. "*No!*" The word squeezed from my body with a gut-wrenching cry. "I told you not to take them on the water!"

I jumped to my feet and my trembling hands wiped the tears from my face. I began to walk the beach, but Henry got to his feet and grabbed my arm. I spun around and slapped him in the face.

"I *told* you," I screeched.

"Dianna," he pleaded. "I'm so sorry. I don't know what happened. We didn't even go out far. Not enough for a wave like that."

"No!" I beat my fists against his chest. "Why didn't you *listen* to me?"

"Dianna, we'll find them!" he assured me as he fought to control his tone. He coughed out the last of the saltwater from his lungs. "Go call the police. I'll search the shoreline."

I continued to hit him harder, but my tiny fists were no match for his hardened chest. They didn't even seem to phase him. Anger boiled in my gut and spread throughout my body. There was no finding them. Not here. Not on this beach, in this time. They were... gone. I purged every emotion from my body until I wasn't strong enough to stand. I collapsed at Henry's feet in a heap of cries and wails. He fell with me, helpless and confused, holding me in his arms, refusing to let me go even though I had taken my anger out on him.

"They're gone," I muttered through sobs. "M-my babies are gone!"

* * *

I sat on the cold wet sand and I watched, unblinkingly, as the sun set over the water. Calm little waves lapped at the rocky shore, barely loud enough to cover the sounds of Henry's approaching footsteps, time and time again. He tried to pry me from the beach and convince me to come up to the house to get warm. But I couldn't bring myself to look at him let alone be in the same house. The last words I spoke to my husband were to tell him not to call the police.

There was no point.

My tears had long dried to my face and I could feel my sticky skin pulling with each flicker of movement. I desperately needed to dry off and get warm, I wasn't a fool. I could feel the chilly Spring mist seeping into my bones. But I couldn't bring myself to be peeled off that beach. I screamed at the water for hours, hoping the siren would rear its head. But the only life to be seen for miles was that of a few seagulls.

Footsteps were approaching again. This time, two sets. I didn't bother to turn and look, they'd be by my side in a matter of time. I had no idea what I could say to them, to explain my behaviour lately. To justify not wanting to call the police. I saw no other way around it. I had to tell Mom and Henry about the siren.

I felt my mother's careful hand slide across my damp back as she hunched down next to me.

"Dianna, baby," her voice calm and soothing. "You have to come up out of the cold. Get something to eat." She paused, perhaps to glance at Henry who stood cautiously behind me. "Maybe we could try calling the police?"

I shook my head.

"Dianna, they can help us find them," she

pushed. "The longer we wait -"

"No," I croaked. "No one can find them."

Henry moved forward, flanking my side and kneeled down in the sand with me. I couldn't look him in the face. He reached for my hand, but I pulled it away. Fresh tears began swelling in my eyes.

"Dianna, you can't ignore me forever," he said. "I'm absolutely gutted over what happened today. I know it's all my fault. But I searched the waters for hours. It's time to call the police to at least..." his voice broke with oncoming tears. "At least find their... b-bodies."

The man I loved was falling apart at my side and I couldn't bear to look at him. To face it. Because the thing was, Henry may have brought them out to the water, but it was my fault the siren wanted them. I could have said something, done something before it was too late. But I was a coward and now I've paid the ultimate price. I just couldn't face the truth yet.

"We're not calling the police," I said again. "They won't find them. Not," I inhaled deeply and squeezed the cold tears from my eyes. "Not in this time."

"What?" they said in unison.

My mouth trembled as I urged the words to come out. To finally face what I'd been lying to myself, and everyone I loved, about.

"The siren came to me a few months ago," I whispered. "Demanding I hold up my end of some stupid bargain."

My mom tensed and covered her mouth to stifle a gasp. "What did it want?"

Finally, I craned my sore neck and looked at her. Her grief matched mine, mixed with an expression of disbelief.

"She wanted me to go back."

"For what reason?" Henry asked.

I shrugged. "She wouldn't say, just kept insisting I had to come back. Eventually, she grew impatient with me. She... took Audrey that day on the beach. As a warning."

Henry went stiff and I could feel him staring daggers into me. Still, I couldn't look.

"You mean," he shot to his feet and looked down at me. "You knew this was going to happen?"

Finally, I dared meet his gaze and I regretted it immediately. "I told you not to take them out on the God damn water!"

His arms flapped helplessly at his sides as he began pacing in front of me, kicking the sand furiously. "I thought you were just nervous after Audrey disappeared."

"I *was*."

Henry guffawed. "Clearly."

Mom continued to rub my back. "Now is not the time to place blame. If what you say is true, then you need to find a way to the past. Tell the siren you'll come back."

"I tried," I told them. "All day I've been yelling at the damn water. Giving in. Waiting for it to show."

Mom let out a frustrated moan. "Those meddlesome beasts. When will it be enough?"

"I can't believe you let me suffer with this grief and guilt *all* day," Henry yelled at me. "You made me think it was all *my* fault! You let me think they were *dead*, for Christ's sake!"

I glared up at him. "I'm in shock. I know that's not an excuse. But what do you want me to say?"

"*I'm sorry* would be a nice start!"

Anger festered in my chest, paralyzing me. I couldn't relent. I couldn't give in and face the truth of my part of the fault. I said nothing and buried my head in my hands as I curled my knees up.

I'm sure there were a million things running through his mind that he wanted to say. Names he wanted to call me. Hurtful words he wanted to throw at me. But, like the good man Henry is, he let out an angry, guttural scream at the water instead, before turning and storming off back to the house. Leaving me there on the beach to suffer in my own grief. To sit with what I had done.

To crumble as my mother sat there and watched helplessly.

What a mess I've made of our perfect little life.

CHAPTER FIVE

I ran stressed fingers through my disheveled hair as I struggled to take a deep breath. It felt as though I hadn't fully inhaled all day. My bottom was beginning to feel numb from sitting on the cold porch, but I couldn't be around Henry right now. I managed to peel myself from the beach at the insistence of my mother and headed up to the house to get cleaned up. But the moment he came back inside, I had to leave. I couldn't handle the tension between us. It didn't feel right.

But it demanded to be there.

I heard the front door close behind me and Mom's footsteps carefully make their way towards me. A steaming cup of broth was stuck in front of my face and I grimaced.

"Eat something," she said curtly.

I took the cup and my body responded immediately to the warmth that spread through my hands. I held it to my chest and closed my eyes. Mom took a seat at my side, her bad leg stuck out straight as she rubbed at it. The eternal reminder of what secrets lay in our pasts. Her own daughter tried to kill her. A fact she couldn't possibly forget. No matter how much she wanted to.

"You must decide what to do, Dianna," she told me. "I know it's hard, I know you're feeling pretty broken right now. But, somewhere out there, a siren has your children."

My lips trembled as I fought back the wave of guilt that rushed over me at her words. "I know."

"You have to go back, baby."

I nodded. But that meant talking to Henry. I wiped away a rogue tear and looked at my mother. "Will you come?"

She shook her head. "No. My time travelling days are over." Her fingers continued to rub at the deadened nerves in her leg. "When Maria threw me to the future, the paramedics found me dead. Did I ever tell you that?"

I didn't reply.

"I'd lost far too much blood. It was nothing short of a miracle that they were able to revive me. I'm grateful for the second chance at life, but I'm almost certain it's why the witches and sirens have let me be. I've died. That life is gone, the ties it held to the threads of time no longer apply." She placed a comforting hand on my back and smiled. "We worked far too hard to build this life here. I'll stay behind and keep it alive. I'll make sure you have a home to come back to."

My eyes filled with tears and I let my head fall to her shoulder. "Thanks, Mom." We sat in silence for a few moments before I finally spoke again. "Do you think it's the witches again? Trying to correct the sanctity of time?"

Mom inhaled a thoughtful breath. "No. It doesn't make sense. The kids are people of this time, and so are you. If they were going to pull anyone back it would have been Henry. Something else is afoot." She shook her head and clucked her tongue. "Wretched beasts. The siren has other motives. But one thing I'm certain of." She shifted and took my free hand in both of hers. "Arthur and Audrey are alive. The siren had wanted you to come back first, so it's *you* they truly want. They won't give up the only leverage they have. They may be dreadful creatures, but they honor and covet bargains."

I set the mug down on the porch and rubbed my warmed hands over my chilly face. "I guess that's some good news in all this damn mess."

"How will you do it?" she asked. "The sun and moon on the water?"

I shook my head and sat up straight. "The siren gave me a pearl."

She released my hand from her grip and

nervously crossed her arms in her lap. "I see. Well, it looks like you have everything you need. Go as soon as possible," Mom replied. "Bring those grandbabies back to me."

I stood up, my back cracked from hours of sitting and wallowing. "Tell anyone who asks that Henry and I took the kids for a trip."

Mom pulled herself to her feet and stared me square in the face with a sense of pride. "When you get there, be careful who you talk to. And never trust the sirens. They can say one thing and mean another. Their words are often mixed with deceit and ill-intent."

"Okay," I replied. The reality of it all was finally starting to catch up with me as my breath hitched.

"The island won't really be settled for another decade but there will be ports there for fishermen, and a boat you can borrow."

Mom held both my shoulders tightly and we stared into one another's tear-filled gaze.

"I love you as much as a human being could possibly love another," she told me. I could only afford a nod and she kissed my cheek before letting me go. "Be safe. And, for the love of God, talk to your poor husband. He's just as crushed as you are, but you're all he has in this world besides those two kids."

I still had no response for my mother, my mind was already in the past. Waiting for my body to show up. I watched as she walked down the few steps of my porch and get in her car. I waved as she sped off and, when the car was out of sight, I turned to head inside to face the man that awaited and the reality of what we had to do.

I found him in the dining room off the kitchen, staring out the picture window that showed the tumultuous ocean expanse in our backyard. His back to me, I caught the moment his body stiffened at my presence. He slowly craned his neck and peered at me across the room.

"Come to place some more blame?" he asked spitefully.

The skin around his dark eyes was reddened from crying. His expression defeated. It took years to build this man up from the broken Devil Eyed Barret to the warm and loving Henry I married. And now, in less than a day, I'd kicked the legs out from underneath him and he was crashing.

"No," I croaked. "I've come to discuss our game plan. We need to go back as soon as possible."

He fully turned to face me, his gaze deep and shadowed by his brow. "The moment the sun and moon meet on the water tomorrow evening, I'll be gone."

He may as well have punched me in the gut for how I suddenly felt. I reached into my pocket and pulled out the pearl, showing it to him in my upturned palm. "We don't have to wait until tomorrow. We can go right now."

Henry's face twisted with confusion and disbelief as he stared at the wish in my hand. Then, with a deep breath, his gaze pierced right through me. He was pissed all over again and I realized why. I'd had the ticket to the past in my grasp all day and said nothing. Anyone else in my position would surely have tossed the thing in the water the second their children went missing. But I've been frozen in my own grief for hours. Unsure if I could even trust the enchanted relic.

"I know I should have told you about the siren," I admitted. "And this pearl. But I lost my mind today. I wasn't thinking straight, I was thinking at all."

He heaved a sigh. "I should have listened when you said not to take them on the water."

I waved off his admission. "Regardless of who's at fault, we have to go back. Right now. We can be mad at one another after we've saved our children." My gaze dropped to the floor. "We need to prepare for the journey."

Henry walked across the room, passing me by without so much as a look or touch, and grabbed his jacket from the rack by the front door. "Grab some gloves. I'll get the shovels."

***

After I packed a bag full of modern necessities we'd surely need, Henry and I trudged off in silence through the thick woods on the other side of our house. It'd been years since we buried the memories of our past, but I knew the very spot we left the trunk. Under a giant maple with a heart-shaped knot. How fitting at the time. But now, I wasn't so sure. Henry and I had made a promise to one another, to bury everything that could possibly be turned into relics for time travel and never speak of it again. Never let the dangers of our past touch the lives of our children. But what good that did. Fate had its grip around our souls, and I wondered when it would stop meddling in our lives.

Maybe it never would.

Perhaps the actions of my mother and sister have forever fused us to the laws of time and fate. Destined to bend to it until our dying days. I shook the dark thoughts from my mind.

The tree appeared in the distance, the moon highlighting the unique marker in the bark. Henry must have remembered too because he came to a stop a few feet ahead and plunged the tip of the spade into the ground. He wasted no time in digging up the forest floor and I stopped for a moment to stare in stunned awe at his tall frame. How it loomed over the hole he dug, the muscles of his wide shoulders moving like parts of a machine. It's like I'd forgotten just how large of a man Henry truly was.

I flanked his side and joined in the digging. Silence wrapped us tightly. The only sounds to be heard were that of the forest and our labored breaths between each pierce of the ground. Until I heard the distinct clank of metal on metal and we both came to a halt. We exchanged a quick glance before Henry dropped to the ground. He moved the last bit of earth from atop the trunk and began to pull it from its grave. I grabbed a side and helped move it to the surface and we stopped to catch our breaths.

Still, silence.

We'd thrown the key in the sea years ago, so Henry took the shovel and smashed the rusted lock. It crumbled to bits and shattered on the ground with a grinding sound. Wordlessly, Henry motioned with his head for me to open it. I bent down and wiped away the crust of dirt in the cracks and pried the lid open. Immediately, I was met with a waft of various scents, all carrying memories of the past. The dank musk of a ship. Dried seawater. Old metal. The stench of smoke from a fire.

Henry reached inside and plucked something from the collection of belongings and shook it out. His black leather trench coat. Billows of dust floated in the air as he slipped his long arms inside the sleeves and I stared frozen as the simple addition of a garment completely transformed him from my husband into the brooding pirate I once knew. How it fit every line and curve of his body as if the memory of his shape had forever been embedded in the very fibers of the fabric. Like a second skin.

Henry's dark gaze held mine as his fingers worked to tie the mess of blonde hair back at the nape of his neck. "Well? What are you waiting for? Grab your stuff and let's get out of here."

I blinked away the fog and peered inside the box.

My eyes landed on familiar red linen, folded neatly on top of my old shoulder bag. I pulled at the red pirate jacket I'd stolen from my sister and copied Henry in shaking out the years of dust and dirt. And, like his, the coat slipped over my body like a missing piece of a puzzle.

Hurriedly, I began stuffing the other items from inside the trunk into my newer bag; a compass, my dagger, a satchel of silver and gold, another bag of gems. We'd need all the help we could get, and all the bargaining tools possible. My fingers wrapped around the hilt of my sword and I pushed myself to my feet to tighten the sheath belt around my waist.

Henry sheathed his blade at his side and looked at me. "Are you ready?"

I secured my sword in its case under my coat and took a deep, nervous breath. "We don't really have a choice, do we?"

CHAPTER SIX

After we rummaged through the rest of the contents in the trunk and filled our bags with everything we needed, Henry and I began our trek back through the woods toward our home. As we crossed the gravel driveway, I came to a halt.

"Hold on," I told him. "I need to grab one more thing inside."

He said nothing but I was met with an impatient glare as he stood and crossed his arms in wait. I ran inside the house and upstairs where my journal sat in my bedside table. Not only did it contain all the best moments of my life over the last four years, but it had pictures of the kids that might help us in finding them. Most were far too modern to reveal to anyone in the past but there was one, in particular, I could use.

Last summer, when the fair came through town, they had a portrait studio where you could dress up in old fashioned garb and have a picture taken. Henry and I took the kids and dressed up as pirates. The end result was a Photoshopped sepia image that could pass as an old Polaroid. Although, I wasn't even sure if cameras were around in the 1700s.

I didn't have time to check.

I stuffed the journal inside a sealed Zip-loc bag and tucked it away in my satchel. When I stepped outside, Henry was leaning against the side of the house in wait. His long black leather coat draped from his tall stature and he peered up at me with those dark eyes. In a day, my sweet Henry was gone and in his place was this new, vengeful version of the brooding pirate captain I once knew. All Henry ever wanted in this world was a simple life, and a family to love. I gave that to him, but I was also responsible for it being ripped away. His anger was expected, but part of me worried if he'd ever be able to forgive me.

"Ready?" I said.

Again, Henry had nothing to say but shoved off from the side of the house and turned on his heel to lead the way down to the water. I followed him in silence, my mind awash with so many thoughts.

Too many. Worries for my children, for our own lives and what we were about to do. I had put this life behind me long ago. Yet, here we were, digging it back up and diving right in headfirst.

We came to a stop on the sand and Henry regarded me coldly. "Where should we do it?"

I scanned around the line where the incoming tide lapped at the mix of sand and rocks. "Over there," I said and pointed at the little jut-out of stone where I found the pearl in the first place.

We carefully stepped across the slick rocks and stood at the very tip. Henry, no matter how mad at me, was still the chivalrous gentlemen and took my hand to help me over. But he shook free his grip the second we came to a halt. With shaky fingers, I reached inside my jacket pocket and pulled out the white pearl. It caught the glimmer of moonlight and shone like a diamond in my palm. Just like the enchanting, scaly skin the siren sometimes took form in.

"Henry," I said and cleared my throat. "Mom warned me about the sirens."

He guffawed. "A little too late, don't you think?"

"No, I mean we have to be careful around them. They're tricky and unpredictable. Their motives are fleeting from one moment to the next. We can't trust anything they say."

He pursed his lips as he stared at me. "Noted."

I sighed as I rolled the pearl around between my fingers. "And she also told me something about the witches," I added sadly. "Martha, and her sisters, they're like timekeepers, of sorts."

His brow pinched together in confusion. "What do you mean?"

I shook my head. "I'm not a hundred percent sure, but Mom said that they're tasked with protecting the sanctity of time. It's why Mom was pulled back. She didn't belong here."

"But they allowed her to come back in the end," Henry pointed out. "When your sister tried to kill her."

"No, Maria *did* kill her," I told him. "When the paramedics found Mom here on the beach, she was technically dead. They revived her. It's like some weird loophole, I guess."

"Why are you telling me this?" he asked, still confused. "*Now*."

Tears wet my eyes and I looked away, cast my gaze out over the evening water. The wind whipped around us, tangling my hair and flapping the long bottoms of our pirate coats.

"You," I said quietly, "I brought you back here with me. But you didn't..."

"I didn't die," he finished for me and slowly gazed up at the moon, realization working its way into his thoughts. "You think I may be stuck in the past if I go back."

I offered a shaky nod.

"Is that something you can accept?" I asked. "I mean, I would understand if it's even something you want -"

"You think I long for that life?" he quickly cut in;

his tone tinged with hurt.

"I don't know what I think anymore, Henry." I fought back the tears that refused to go away.

He turned from me and pushed his tense fingers through his hair as he stood before the sea. I could see the weight of everything on his shoulders and how his entire body seemed to battle with itself, with the emotions he must be feeling. I felt them, too. We weren't in a good place and our children were lost in another time.

"You want to know what I think?" he said intently and spun around; his eyes wide with anguish. "I can't believe you'd even ask me such a thing. That you'd assume what we have isn't good enough for me. Have I not been happy? Have I not been content?" I hung my head in shame as he continued. "I was perfectly fine with the warm and comfortable little life we've built here. Until it was all turned upside down. Something that *you* had a hand in, may I remind."

"Henry." I choked on the words before they had a chance to escape.

He pointed at me, tears in his broken gaze. "I could have helped you. We could have worked together to prevent this from happening. I would have gladly taken our entire life and moved it as far away from here as possible to keep those children safe. I would have done anything for them, for *you*. If you'd just *told* me."

His anger grated against my very soul and regret seared under the surface of my skin. I bit back the tears and rage I harbored at myself and took a deep breath. "Well, it's too late for all that now, isn't it?" I held up the pearl between the tips of my fingers and Henry glared at it.

"Just do it," he said with defeat.

I secured my footing on the slippery rock and tossed the enchanted pearl into the ocean. We stood together, a tangible space between us, and watched as the little bead began to dissipate. A circle of shimmering facets pulsed from its center. For a moment, my mind scrambled for the right words. I couldn't just wish for my kids back. The siren wouldn't have it. She demanded I return to the past and gave me the pearl to do just that. If I wanted any chance at saving my children, I had no choice but to listen and not do anything to further anger the beast.

"I wish to go back," I swallowed hard and quickly added, "To a time where my children are."

We both held our breath as we peered down to watch the last of the pearl dissolve. My heart beat wildly as the last of it disappeared, the sparkles sinking below the surface of the water. Silence filled the air and my chest tightened in disbelief.

Nothing happened.

"What?" I whispered in shock. My eyes bulged as panic filled my body. "No, no. This is what you wanted! Take me! I'm here!"

The words suddenly died in my throat as I noticed the water changing. A few yards out, the ocean began to move in a circular motion. Waves crashed together as a cyclone formed, drawing in more and more water as it grew before us. Henry and I stepped back and craned our necks as we ogled the massive wave that took shape and hovered above us, almost like it were… waiting.

The water flexed as it seemed to take a deep breath and solidify while it reared back. It took me a second to realize what was happening, but Henry was already one step ahead of me.

"Dianna!" he bellowed loudly as the body of water flung itself toward us with a titanic force.

The ground beneath our feet shook and Henry grabbed me in a tight embrace, wrapping his entire body around mine. The cyclone crashed down on top of us with a strength unlike anything I'd ever felt. More powerful than a storm, or any force of nature. The power of time and magic collided and we hurled into a watery abyss together. I could feel the strain we fought against as the waves worked to separate us.

His arms and legs shook as they struggled to keep their hold around me. Something was wrong. I felt his lips press against the side of my face and my fingers reached for him as he was ripped from me. My mouth gaped with a scream, allowing water to pour inside and I choked for air. The tumultuous power of the ocean severed us, dragging Henry away kicking and reaching for me until I could no longer see him. Darkness closed in and I drifted off, deeper and deeper underwater to the chilling depths of the sea…

... and time.

CHAPTER SEVEN

The sound of heavy, wet boots clunking across hollow boards crashed against the cawing of seagulls and scrambled my foggy brain. I pried open one eye only to be blinded by the blaring sun directly above. I was flat on my back, too stiff and sore to move. People bustled right by me as if I weren't even lying on the ground at their feet.

With a hefty moan, I raised my head and squinted to peer around. I was on a boardwalk. The stench of fish floated in the air and salty sea mist drenched my skin. The footsteps belonged to men—fishermen—and I was in their way as they worked to unload crates of fish.

I tried to move, to even stand, but my mind spun in fast circles with every breath I took. My hand shot up to brace my head as I slumped back down to the ground and it came away with a sticky substance all over my palm. Blood. I touched the wound again, to assess the damage, and I was losing blood. Fast. My leg ached, but I could move it. It wasn't broken.

Thank God.

"What are you doin' down there, dearie?" an old man stopped to ask. His accent almost seemed French. He pulled a small wooden wheelbarrow full of fish and set it down before kneeling at my side. He eyeballed my head wound and clucked his tongue. "Nasty cut you got there."

My throat burned as I attempted to speak. "Yeah, uh, have you seen…" My head whirled again, and I slammed back to the ground behind me. "Have you seen a man? My husband. He was… just with me."

The old guy craned his neck and searched around us. "No, you're all alone, m'love. Are you alright?"

My fingers came away from my forehead with fresh crimson. "No, I think I hit my head pretty good."

He stood and reached out his hands. "Here, let's get you on your feet and up to the house. The wife will get you fixed up in no time."

I took his offer and let him help me up. His arm shot around my back and I couldn't help but let my weight fall to him. But he didn't falter. The old guy was solid. Built like the hard-working men of the past. I glanced around again, to take stock of my surroundings. Old rickety boardwalk where half a dozen little punts were tied up. A handful of weary, but happy, fishermen. They all wore knitted sweaters and pulled wooden dollies; the expanse of land to my right showed a small community of quaint cottage-like houses. Smoke billowed from the crooked chimneys.

I did it. I made it back.

"But my husband -"

"What does he look like?" the old fisherman asked as he patiently walked with me. My limp slowed us down. "I'll ask around."

"Pale yellow hair, most likely pinned back. Long black jacket. Goes by the name Henry." I threw a glance over my shoulder. "What about your fish?"

He brushed it off with the wave of a hand. "I'll come back for it."

My head had suddenly gone from woozy to swimming and the weight of a concussion forced me down. The world around me spun wildly until my body smacked the hard ground. The last thing I remember was the old guy calling for help.

I awoke sometime later, my body protesting too much to truly stay asleep. The fog was back, and I struggled to remember what happened or where I was. My eyes fluttered open to find a small room, brightly lit by the afternoon sun, a handmade quilt thrown over me. My clothes and bag neatly folded and stacked on a wooden chair by my side.

A knock at the door alerted me and I struggled to

sit up. An older woman with grey curls tucked back in a classy bun entered the room. She carried a tray of food; some kind of soup and a cup of tea.

"Figured you might be waking up soon and I thought to bring you something warm to eat," she said. Her voice reminded me of Aunt Mary, raspy and sweet. Motherly. It made me miss her greatly.

"Thanks," I replied and let my back rest against the pillow propped behind me. "I'm sorry, who are you? And... where am I?"

The woman chuckled. "My husband found you down by the dock. You took quite a fall it seems."

My fingers felt for the bloody gash but only found a cleaned wound, stitched and bandaged. I looked at her curiously and she grinned.

"I was a nurse in England," she explained quaintly and set the tray down on a small table. "Before we moved to Newfoundland."

"Can you tell me where I am?" I asked her. Her brow pinched together in confusion. I feigned a laugh. "I think I hit my hit a little too hard. I'm just a bit disoriented."

She patted my leg over the covers. "Of course. You're in Donlong. James is out asking around about your husband now."

Donlong? I'd never heard of that town before. Then again, Newfoundland has changed the names of so many places over the years, it was hard to tell. I could be anywhere. "James?" I repeated. "Is that your husband?"

She stood in the doorway and turned to me. "Yes,

the one who found you yesterday. Lucky he did. You surely would have fallen off the side of the dock and drowned."

I was no stranger to that.

"I'll leave you be," she said. "Get some more rest. You're welcome to stay as long as you need."

Rest was the last thing I needed with this concussion. I'd slept far too long as it was. But my body ached from the beating it took. The second she closed the door, I reached for my bag. Everything was still there and intact and I sighed a breath of relief. I quickly pulled out the Advil bottle and popped two pills before stuffing it all back in the bag.

I sat there in a strange bed, in a strange house, as the silence of the room closed in on me. My mind threatened to succumb to the beckon of sleep, but I knew I had to stay awake for as long as possible. I'd already spent the night asleep and I was lucky I even woke up at all. I was no doctor, but I could feel the severity of this head wound. I had to take it easy.

But my nerves got the best of me in no time and I flung the blankets to the side and tipped my legs over the edge of the bed. Henry was missing in addition to my kids. I couldn't just lie around and wait for something to happen. With a deep breath, I grabbed my things and suffered through every simple move I mustered.

I made my way out to the main area of the house. The warmth of a blazing fire in a stone hearth warmed my skin, but my footsteps echoed off the empty walls. I spotted the woman outside in the yard, hanging wet sheets on the line. She looked up when I opened the back door and I let it fall shut behind me.

"Couldn't sleep, dearie?"

I shook my head and grasped the thick strap of my shoulder bag. "I need to find my husband and get on my way. But I appreciate everything you've done for me. Thank you, truly."

She finished pinning the last sheet and turned to me. "Well, James has been asking around all morning and hasn't heard a thing. If a newcomer showed up in the Donlong as you did, we'd surely hear of it."

"Donlong," I said curiously. "That's on the West Coast?" I took a stab in the dark.

She regarded me with confusion again. She probably thought I belonged in bed; a strange girl who didn't even know where she was. "Sorry, I'm just lost. My husband and I were traveling from..." Rocky Harbour had yet to exist and I scrambled for words. "North. I'm just trying to get my bearings."

She bent down and grabbed the empty wicker laundry basket. "You're correct. We're Donlong the point. On the West Coast of Newfoundland."

She must have thought I was nuts. I smiled and played off my nerves. "I'm sorry, I never did get your name." I stuck out my hand. "I'm Dianna."

She gladly shook it. "Jacintha."

"I'm going to wander around town, maybe take a

walk around the shoreline to see if I can find my husband." I swallowed against the sudden strain in my throat. "Or... for some sign of him. Would it be alright if I came back here tonight? If I find nothing, I'll be moving on in the morning. And I can pay you for -"

"Now, now," she said quickly, almost offended. "You'll be doing no such thing. Keep your money. You're more than welcome to stay as long as you want."

I sighed in relief. "Thank you."

Jacintha walked past me toward the house and turned before she went inside. "I'll put some supper up for you. Be careful on the shores. It's rocky."

The flimsy screened door slammed closed behind her and I was off. I spent the rest of the day stopping locals and asking questions about a stranger who looked like Henry but all I found were pitiful nods and empty replies. All anyone heard about was my arrival. A wayward woman on her own, waking up on the docks, confused and wounded. If this town were big enough for a newspaper, I'd be front-page news.

I took my time and combed the shoreline as far as I possibly could. Looking under fallen tree roots, venturing inside small caves, around the crevices of boulder clusters. But my husband was nowhere to be found. After hours of searching, I plopped down on a rock to rest, not realizing just how much precious energy I was spending until I stopped. I struggled to catch my breath and my brain was so tired. My leather boots toed the wet sand as the ocean crashed in small, loud waves against the jutting stones. Taunting me.

"You think you're so smart," I said and narrowed my eyes at the water. "Forcing my hand and messing with my mind, making me come back here." I picked up a pebble and threw it out a way. "I don't understand what you're doing. You demanded I come back. You took my kids when I wouldn't listen. Separated me from Henry." I stood and flapped my arms helplessly at my sides. "I'm here, God damn it! What else do you want from me? What's the point of all this?"

The air in my lungs tightened as I caught the faintest sight of movement on the water as if something swam just below the surface. Was the siren finally showing its face? My chest pinched as I held my breath and inched closer, unblinking. Ripples cascaded out from a pinpoint and I waited anxiously. But all that emerged was the pebble I'd just thrown in the water; it flicked through the air and bounced off my jacket. Rage seared through my body and I let out a fierce scream. Like a madwoman, I bent down to grab handfuls of rocks and pelted them at the sea, over and over until my arms ached and I collapsed to the cold, wet ground in defeat.

I couldn't even muster a tear, I felt entirely empty. Lost.

The sun was just starting to go down by the time I

wrenched myself from the ground and headed back to James and Jacintha's home. I was eternally grateful for their help since my arrival, but I would have to leave. I had to go out in search of Henry and the kids myself because it was pretty clear that the siren was playing some game that I wasn't in on. Or I wasn't quite passing some twisted test she had me up against.

When I approached the little white picket fence that surrounded their home, I found James sitting outside in a rocking chair, whittling some piece of wood. He glanced up at me and I hoped he couldn't see the despair on my face.

"Still no luck finding that man of yours?" he asked.

I stopped and leaned against the railing. "No. Did you hear anything around town?"

He shook his head sadly. "No, dear. I'm afraid not. And, believe me, if a stranger by the likes of the gentleman you described showed up, I'd surely hear about it by now."

I inhaled deeply. "I'm going to have to head out and expand my search."

"Well, you'll be needing some help," James replied. "And transport. I'm afraid I'm tied up with my duties aboard the rig. I can't leave. But I'm happy to give you a ride to where you need."

He was right. I'd need all the help I could get if I were going to find Henry and the kids. And there were very few I could trust. I was hoping I could slip in and out of the past without alerting my old crew of our arrival. It damn near killed me to leave them before. I wasn't sure I could do it again.

But what choice did I have?

"James, do you know of a ship called The Queen?"

The old man's face lit up. "Of course, everyone does. The crew was gone for years, only just returned a few months ago." He examined my face closer than he had before and recognition flashed across his expression. His finger pointed and wagged at me as he formulated his thoughts. "I knew I recognized your face. You're the Pirate Queen, ain't you?"

I forced my face to remain staid and shook my head. "No, you have me mistaken. I know the crew from many years ago, and I'm sure they could help me. Where would I find them?"

He chuckled. "Just over Uplong. Not far. On the other side of Sandy Point."

That caught my attention. "Sandy Point?" I inched loser. "You mean I've been in Sandy Point this whole time?"

James looked at me with a dumbfounded look. How strange he must think me to be.

"Yes, dearie," he replied slowly. "This is Donlong the point. The crew of The Queen has been docked Uplong the point for months. Don't know what they're doing over there, but the ship hasn't moved in weeks."

I chuckled helplessly. I felt like an idiot. I knew the area had been divided between the Catholics and

Anglicans for centuries. *Up along* and *down along* the point. I knew exactly where I was now.

"Up along the point, is that where the Thirsty Trout is?" I asked him.

He smiled with delight. "Yes, yes, it is. Lovely little tavern. Is that where you're going?" he asked. "Do you know it?"

I nodded. "Can you bring me?"

Finally, a break. I knew the Trout well. After all, it was the very place I went from a being prisoner of pirates to a member of the crew aboard The Devil's Heart. It's where all this began.

The moment I fell in love with Captain Devil Eyed Barrett.

Henry had to be there.

CHAPTER EIGHT

I couldn't wait until morning. Thankfully, James was willing to saddle up his horse and bring me across the point, to the other side where the larger population of people had settled. The docks were bigger, busier. The houses were plentiful. Familiar, as I took in the emerging rooftops that trimmed the horizon. We came to a stop just outside a tavern nestled between other storefronts; a bakery and a convenience store of sorts. It was late, and everything was closed. All except the one with the hand-carved sign out front that read The Thirsty Trout. Memories flooded my mind as I flung my leg over the side of the horse and hopped to the ground.

"You be safe now," James warned me as he peered down from his mount. "I hope you find your husband."

"Thank you," I replied. "For everything. I'll forever be in your debt." I reached into my bag and pulled out a few gold coins. "Here."

The old man held up a hand and shook his head. "Absolutely not. What kind of Christian man would I be if I accepted payment for doing the right thing?"

"It's not payment," I insisted and pressed the coins into his palm. "It's a thank you."

He smiled appreciatively and gave me one curt tip of his flat cap before kicking his heels. The horse turned around and I stood there and watched as he trotted off through town. When he was out of sight, I spun and faced the tavern before me. Distant memories poured to the forefront of my brain. With a deep breath, I opened the door and walked inside.

The place was quiet, and not one thing had changed in the years since my last visit. The old wooden floors still bowed in areas, matching the rustic hand-carved trunks of trees used to support the ceiling above. A few guests sat around the fireplace near the back.

"Dianna?" a familiar voice spoke softly.

I turned to the front desk to find Nathaniel, the sweet old innkeeper who had treated me like family. And, according to the records I'd dug up when searching for the fates of our friends,

Nathaniel Sheppard was, indeed, a distant ancestor of mine on my father's side. He was family, just as I had suspected when we first met. My blood ties to this past. A root I could actually be proud of.

I grinned from ear to ear. "Hi, Nathaniel. It's good to see you."

He set his spectacles down on the wooden counter and scuttled around to the front with open arms. "I would say that's quite the understatement. It's so wonderful to see you after all these years." I let him wrap me in a quick embrace. "What are you doing here?"

"I'm looking for my old crew," I told him. "From The Devil's Heart. They're sailing The Queen now."

He nodded thoughtfully. "Yes, I've seen them around town. They come and go, but the ship is down by the docks. Empty, for the most part. As far as I can tell."

Empty? That didn't make any sense. Where were they all staying?

"Have you seen or heard from Captain Barrett? Henry?" I asked, hopeful.

He pondered a moment "No, I'm afraid not. Is he meeting you here?"

My stomach twisted in a knot. "I'm... not sure. We were separated in our travels. Do you have a room I can rent for a few nights?"

"Now, *that* I can help with," he said and walked back behind the desk. He ducked down and came back up with a set of keys. "You just missed supper, but I can have the wife warm something up for you if you like."

I took the keys and stuffed them in my jacket pocket. "Spaghetti?" I asked teasingly.

Nathaniel laughed. "No, rabbit stew. But I think tomorrow's the perfect day for the pasta special. Perhaps I could get your help in the kitchen? We've replicated your wonderful recipe hundreds of times, but it's still not as good as the one made by your hand."

I felt a rush of pride and warmth in his presence. Maybe it was knowing we shared the same blood. Or maybe it was his loveable personality. Regardless, I was grateful this man existed in a time when I needed all the help I could get.

"I'd love to."

"Excellent!" he cried happily. "You go get settled in your room upstairs now and I'll have the wife bring up a tray for you."

I covered his hand with mine and gave it a squeeze. He regarded me with a sparkle in his eye, the same way my father's used to catch the light when he looked at me. I wished I could tell this man we were family. To share that with him. But I knew I couldn't disrupt the sanctity of time any more than I already have.

He waited for me to say something, but I just gave his hand a quick pat and then headed upstairs. The room was just like all the others and exactly how I remembered. Quaint, peaceful, and dimly lit. A small window, hardly large enough for a child to fit through, allowed a sliver of moonlight. I got a fire going in the little hearth and the room became cast in a warm glow. My weary bones shivered.

I removed my damp socks and hung them over the flames with my jacket and upturned boots. Once they were dry, I was heading down to the docks. I couldn't waste any more time sitting around. And it was evident that the siren wasn't going to tell me my next steps. I had to forge my own and find a way to get my kids back.

And Henry.

Vivid thoughts of the worst-case scenarios constantly flashed across the forefront of my mind. Was he lost? Hurt? Did he lose his memory? Or, worse... was he laying dead somewhere on an empty beach? If only I had some sign that he was at least alive.

I shook the thoughts from my head. I couldn't think like that. Henry *was* alive. And he was out there, just like me, searching. Fighting to get back to me. I had to hold on to that resolve, it was all I had.

Like clockwork, Nathaniel's wife came knocking at the door just as I was slipping on my newly warmed socks. She handed me a tray of reheated stew, some bread, and a cup of tea. I thanked her as she left and closed the door behind her. I was starving, but my eagerness to find The Queen trumped everything so I scarfed down a few bites—cursing when it burned the roof of my mouth—and headed out.

The docks were long emptied of the fishermen and visiting sailors for the day and the boats gently waded in the water, each knocking up against the slick wood with eerie creaks. Like sleeping beasts. My boots crunched the bits of sand and dirt that littered the pier as I passed by a dozen ships and skiffs.

Finally, I stopped and stared at her. The Queen. She sat alone at the end, ready to leave at a moment's notice. The portholes were black, and no sign of life could be found. With a quick look over my shoulder, I ran and jumped aboard, my leather boots slamming on the deck with a loud clunk. I froze for a second, waiting for incoming footsteps, but no one came. I was all alone, a fact that was becoming more and more true with each minute I spent in the past.

I walked the upper deck, hung to the shadows that loomed from overhead as I brushed my fingers along the railing. The same one I fell over during that storm. Before I stumbled upon Benjamin. I turned and headed down by the mizzenmast where Finn used to teach me sparing and swordplay. He gave me such a gift in those months. The ability to defend myself. I wondered then; how rusty I'd become over the years.

Instinctively, my hand went to the sword tucked underneath my jacket and my fingers wrapped around the hilt. I slowly pulled it from the sleeve and admired its beauty. Hefty and long, yet lightweight and made for me. I flicked my wrist and spun the blade in circles while I moved around the deck, swiping and jabbing at the air around me. Images of the kraken attack filled my vision and I remembered it as if it were yesterday.

When I'd had my fun, I returned the weapon to my side and ducked below deck. The mess hall smelled exactly the same; musty mixed with woodstove smoke and cooked meats. The room was pitch black. An old candle sat in a pile of cold, melted wax so I fished a pack of matches from my bag and lit it. The flame didn't offer a ton of light, but enough for me to see how very little had changed since I left.

The same pots and pans still hung from the rack above the sink. A block of knives sat on the butcher top in the center of the room, next to some dried veggies that had clearly been left out too long. I walked behind it and ran my hand along the edge of the countertop on the back wall, the very spot Henry had set his marriage proposal in stone.

Tears filled my eyes, but my heart pulsed painfully as the sound of a clean blade being removed from the wooden block came from behind. I froze, unable to move. Heavy footsteps slowly pursued and stopped at my back. I let out a yelp as the blade came around and pressed against my throat.

"I dinnae ken who ye are but I suggest ye back away and get the hell off my ship, ye filthy wench. Won't be stealing nothin' from The Queen tonight."

A rush of warmth and relief filled me as the familiar voice spoke. I didn't move, the knife was still firmly pressed against my throat after all. But I slowly held up my hands.

"My name's not wench…"

I felt the air thicken as he removed the knife and set it down. When I heard his clunky boots scuffle back, I finally turned around. I knew it was damn near pitch-black down here, but the tiny candle offered the faintest bit of light and it shined off the side of my face, just as it did his. The bushy red beard, the messy ginger waves that hung down from his hat. He hadn't changed a bit. I couldn't stop smiling, even if I wanted to.

"Hello, Finnigan."

The giant Scott stood locked in a wide-eyed stance of disbelief.

"Well?" I urged nervously. "Aren't you going to say something?"

"Ahhhh!" he belted out in a thick Scottish churn. His long arms flung out at his sides, inviting me in. "*Dianna!*"

I fell into his open embrace and Finn squeezed me so tight I thought my ribs would crack. His body shook with laughter and cries of disbelief. I had no idea how good it would feel to see him again. My first friend in this chaotic era. Heck, in my whole existence. Finnigan Artair bonded to me the moment we met and had stuck his neck out for me every chance he got. Ours was a friendship that would stand the test of time. Literally.

Finally, he grabbed my arms and pushed me away, just enough to get a good gawk at me. Breathy and scattered, he looked me up and down.

"What the Christ are ye doin' here?" he asked and pawed at my face as if he still couldn't believe I was standing there. "Are ye alright? Where's the wee one? Where's Henry?"

"That's a bit of a long story," I told him. "But I'm here to ask for your help. And the crew. Where are they?"

He let out a gutsy, raspy moan. "Aye, a lot's changed in four years, Time Traveller." He flung an arm around my shoulder. "Let's get a drink."

CHAPTER NINE

"I can't believe they got married," I said to Finn and took a big gulp of my ale.

We headed back to the Thirsty Trout and Nathaniel was all too happy to have us there. The two of us sat in wingback chairs across from one another as a small fire crackled softly to our right. The rest of the tavern to the left had fallen silent as its guests retreated to their rooms or headed home for the night.

"Aye, 'twas a lovely ceremony, too," he replied. "Small, quick. Just like Lottie wanted it." He chuckled to himself. "Funny watching Gus for weeks, scrambling with his old-fashioned ways. He tried everythin' to convince the lass to have a traditional weddin'. She wouldn't have it, though. Was just us and the pastor on the front lawn of The Siren's Call."

My lips pursed at the mention of the place. Of Roselyn Wallace's home. That woman still left a bad taste in my mouth, even after all these years. How she once held Henry's heart in her hands; it hurt me to think of it.

"Oh, Time Traveller," he said, "Ye need not worry about Roselyn. She's harmless. Did her best to make up for what she did. Put us up for years. Helped us get back home."

I nodded. Sure, I was grateful she took care of my friends after I left. Still... she did aid my psychotic sister in an attempt to kill me and my mother. The fact that she was forced to do it is beside the point.

"So, what made you guys decide to come back?" I asked. "After all this time? Why not just stay in England?"

Finn shrugged and wiped his beard of ale. "Was time. Lottie was... anxious to get home. We'd long overstayed our welcome. And Ben..."

"What about Benjamin?"

Finn seemed to struggle with his words and a ball of Scottish grunts and groans quietly erupted from his throat. "The lad is tortured by his past, Dianna. And this present leaves him unsettled. He was always comin' and goin' like the wind. Even now, he's gone Lord knows where. But he *was* eager to get back here. That much I know."

We fell quiet as I processed everything he told me about their time in England. But there was one detail Finn seemed to purposely avoid. I inhaled deeply through my nose, unsure if I should bring it up. But I had to, I couldn't live the rest of my life not knowing.

"And… my sister's body?" I asked, my gaze hidden under my brow as I focused on the wood grain in the small table between us.

"Burned to a fine crisp, buried in a sealed jar in the middle of the woods," he told me with certainty. I glanced up and met his steady stare as Finn reached across and grasped my hand. "Made sure the devil would never touch the sea again, lass. I promise it."

A ball formed in my throat and I pushed it down with ale. I would not shed a tear for that woman, that monster. She deserved far worse than what she got.

"So, tell me all about the wonders of the future," he said cheerily, an attempt to brighten the dark mood that suddenly fell on our reunion. "Do ye have flying horses yet?"

I laughed. "No, not yet. But… we're happy." Then I rethought that. "I mean, we *were* happy. Until all of this happened."

He shifted to the edge of his seat. "Tell me more. Ye dinnae really explain much."

I shrugged helplessly. "I don't even know where to begin. The siren came to me a few months ago. Demanding I come back for some reason. I'd made a deal with her a long time ago, back when were lost on Shellbed Isle. But I didn't fully understand what I'd gotten myself into by promising the siren a favor. In fact, I'd forgotten all about it until she appeared in the water one evening."

"What did she say?"

"Nothing really," I told him. "Just that I owed her a favor and she wanted me to come back. I refused and she went away. But a few weeks later she came again, and then again, and again. Until one afternoon, one of my kids went missing."

Finn's eyes widened in disbelief.

"It was only for a moment," I assured him. "We found her. But I took it as a warning. And I was right to assume it, because the next chance the siren got, she took both my kids and brought them back here. Forcing me to hold up my end of the bargain."

"Wait," he said and pinched his brow. "*Both* kids?"

I smiled. "Yes, I had twins. Arthur and Audrey." I grabbed my bag and pulled out the journal that contained every milestone of their little lives and showed Finn a picture of them.

"My God," he said and blew out a huff of air. "The wee ones look just like Henry."

I peered at the photograph admiringly and tears swelled in my eyes. "I know. Audrey's most like him, though. Stubborn and brave. Fearless. She loves the ocean."

Finn tipped his head and regarded me kindly.

"Aye, I'd say she's more like her mother, then."

I wiped at a rogue tear that escaped and ran down my cheek.

"Dinnae worry, lass," he said comfortingly. "We'll find Henry and the little ones."

I returned the journal to my bag and gripped it tightly to my chest. "I don't know what's worse. Knowing that the kids are with the siren, or not knowing where Henry is at all. I just wish I knew he was at least alive."

"Ah, the captain is alive. I have no doubt about that," Finn replied and leaned back in his chair. "Never met anyone so brave and strong as he. The things he's survived. Henry will be just fine, lass. All we have to do is find him."

His words did very little to assure me, but I nodded and smiled, anyway.

"I'll need your help," I told him. "All of your help. The whole crew."

Finn grumbled under his breath. "I'm nae sure about Gus, and Ben's been gone for days. But... I ken where Lottie might be found."

"Where?"

He sighed and stood up from the chair. "Ye best just follow me and see for yerself."

***

My boots crunched the half-frozen gravel of the streets, but the sound melted away as my ears filled with the noise of loud men and scuffing chairs. I could hear the jarring commotion of the pub as we approached it from across town. Melodies of fiddles and other Irish instruments laced each bellowing growl of a losing hand of cards. I reached for the wooden handle and recoiled as the crash of furniture screeched against the walls.

"Sounds like the boys are havin' a time," Finn said with glee. He must come here often.

I stepped back and let him haul open the heavy slab door before I followed him inside. The sound amplified immediately and banged against my head. The racket didn't subside, but the attention of the patrons averted right to Finn and I. Dozens of curious eyes fell on me and I tipped the brim of my red hat down over my face. Even though she was long gone, I had to remember that I still resembled my much-hated sister. A target could easily form on my back. I could practically hear the whispers now.

Maria Cobham is back from the dead.

I shuddered and followed closely behind Finn as he sauntered through the pub towards the back where a few men drank merrily while they threw small knives at the wall. When Finn stopped, I peered over his shoulder and saw that they were actually throwing blades at a target; a sloppily painted ring of white circles.

"Anyone care to make this interesting?" a higher-pitched voice spoke up.

I shifted from behind Finn's wide back and sidled

up to him. My gaze traveled through the dense crowd of drunken sailors and locals for the familiar voice and my eyes landed on the back of a blonde head of hair. Her yellow locks fell haphazardly around her exposed shoulders and she turned toward me as she lifted a large mug of ale to her mouth. My eyes widened and remained glued to Lottie, unblinking, as I watched my old friend behave so carelessly. In her half-drunk state, she didn't even realize I was standing right there.

"Who dares brave my aim?" she called out over the swarm.

A sweaty man emerged to the front and swiped the mug from her hands before downing the rest of the contents. Half of it spilled over his dirty face and clothes. Lottie eyed him devilishly as he stumbled to the front and placed his back against the painted circles.

She grinned. "If I strike you, I owe you a hundred silver coins."

"Do your worst," he challenged.

Lottie swung a giant blade in circles with a flick of her wrist as she spun around, facing us, and her eyes met mine for the first time. She stared, gaze wide and blank, chest heaving. I couldn't tell if she was surprised or pissed off at the sight of me. But we stood there for a cold moment, in stunned awe. With a deep breath, Lottie spun back around and flung the knife right at the man on the wall. It zipped by his head and stuck in the wood next to his ear.

Everyone went up in a roar of drunken delight.

Lottie then continued; grabbing knives from the rickety table and flinging them at the brave man in continued succession. She hardly seemed to even pay attention. He stood, back flat against the wall, as she whipped spinning blades him. After seven, she gave up. And the sadistic man stepped away from and outline around his head. He began to walk away, but Lottie grabbed hold of his arm.

"Hey," he said and shook her off.

Lottie advanced a step, a stone-cold look in her eye. "You owe me a hundred silver coins."

"That wasn't the deal," he replied slyly. "You specifically said if you were to strike me, then *you* would owe *me*. Not the other way around."

Without missing a beat, Lottie's hand shot out and her long fingers wrapped around the guy's neck. She squeezed so hard he dropped to his knees in seconds. Then she leaned in and spoke sternly against his face.

"You don't want me squeezing any other part of your body, do you?" Her fingers gripped a smidge harder and the guy's chest tightened. Lottie held out her other hand, palm up. "Coins."

He scrambled with his pockets and pulled out a brown drawstring satchel. Lottie snatched and let him go in one swift movement and he backed away, choking for air.

Lottie bounced the weight of the bag in her hand and glared at the man.

"It's all I have," he told her.

"It'll do. Now get lost."

He ran out of the pub and the crowd around us immediately went on as if it never happened; cheering loudly and smashing mugs of ale together as music played.

Finn glanced down at me, his mouth pursed. "She's... dealing with things."

"What *things*?" I asked, totally stunned, as she neared us. I smiled at my old friend, but she regarded me without expression at all. "It's good to see you."

Lottie fixed her gaze to Finn who sighed guiltily.

"Dianna's back," he said.

"I see that," she replied and looked back at me. "What are you doing here?"

I wanted so desperately to reach out and embrace her, but something told me to stay back.

Finn moaned under his breath. "She needs our help finding Henry."

"Seems like you only come to the past to save that helpless man," Lottie spoke to me. I still couldn't tell if she were happy to see me or not.

I wrought my fingers together.

Lottie sighed heavily and rolled her eyes. "Jesus Christ, come here." She reached for me and I let out a slight laugh of relief. I hugged her tightly, but she quickly stepped away. "You look well."

"Thanks," I replied. "I'm actually not here to find Henry. I mean, I am looking for him. We got separated on the journey back. We're really here to find our kids."

A flicker of something washed over her and she froze. Just for a split second, barely enough for me to see.

"Kids?"

"Yeah," I said and smiled warmly as I thought of their little faces. "A... siren took them. Brought them back here."

Finn leaned in. "She needs us, lass. The crew. We haven't much time. Where's that husband of yers?"

Lottie tore her eyes from mine and grabbed a random mug of ale sitting on a table. She shrugged and then paced the floor. "He went hunting yesterday morning. I haven't seen him since."

"Lottie," I said. She stopped pacing but didn't look at me. "I really need your help. The Queen can't sail without the crew, and I may have to sail to the other side of Newfoundland to find Henry and the kids."

"What do you plan to do?" she asked me.

"I don't quite know," I admitted. "I need to locate the siren in order to find my kids, but I have no idea where Henry could be or how to find him." Emotions bubbled in my gut and I failed to squash them down. My eyes watered as I squeezed my arms over my chest. "So, I guess I start with the siren. I plan to row out on the water tomorrow when the sun meets the moon and ask for the beast to appear."

"And if that doesn't work?" she said curtly.

I shrugged helplessly. "I don't know. I'll figure it

out then. For now, this is all I've got. I *need* you."

Lottie came close, assuring, and rubbed her hand against my back. Her crystal blue eyes glistened and, for a moment, she was the same old Lottie again. Like I could trust her to help. It almost felt like she was on board for a second, but she looked me square in the eye and shook her head.

"I'm sorry for what's happened, and I know you came a long way, but I can't help."

"Lass -"

"I said no, Finnigan!" she urged angrily and refused to face us. She took a deep breath. "You should go."

His mouth gaped to refute but I gently grabbed his arm and tugged. "No, let her be."

It killed me to come all this way only to be rejected by someone I cared so much for. A friend I considered family. But it was evident that there was something wrong with Lottie. Finn was right, four years is a long time. What happened to everyone after we left?

With a thick sigh, Finn turned and walked out the front door with me. I inhaled the fresh night air the second we were outside, and a warm tear escaped, running down my chilly cheek. Gus was off hunting, Lottie was a disaster, Benjamin was nowhere to be found. The crew stopped sailing. But why?

"What..." I shook my head, "What the hell happened to you guys?"

"Too much to explain in one breath," he replied as we strolled down the narrow gravel road toward the Trout. "We're all facing our own demons since returning to Newfoundland. But Lottie's had a harder time than the rest of us. She…"

"Finn," I said quietly and stopped to face him. "What's going on?"

His mouth turned down in a saddened frown. "On the voyage home from England, we were hit with a few storms." His brow arched. "Nothin' of the likes that *we* faced, but ugly, nonetheless. One of the ties came loose one evening when the ship was rockin' in the waves. Lottie ran out to secure it and she stumbled. The railing slammed right into the lass's gut."

The look of confusion on my face prompted him to continue, although he did so with a reluctant sigh.

"She was pregnant."

A cold gasp escaped my throat and my blood ran icy in my veins. A silent cry bubbled up from my stomach as I cupped my hand over my mouth. The tears flowed freely now. My dear friend, the tragic loss she endured aboard the ship. My heart was breaking for her. I fought with the idea to run back.

Finn hung his head. "Aye, it was hard to watch. We still had half our journey ahead, but Lottie already spiraled into darkness. We came down the Northern passage and docked here on the West Coast. She stepped off the ship and hasn't so much as thrown a glance at it since."

"And Gus?" I asked, my voice cracking with grief.

"Poor bugger," Finn replied. "Lottie's shut him

out. Shut everyone out. He's dealin' with it like you'd expect Gus to. In solitude."

"That's not right," I said. "That's a loss like no other. They should be grieving together."

I knew the words to be true, but the moment they spilled from my mouth a sharp squeeze took hold of my heart. It's exactly what I did to Henry. Our kids went missing and I immediately blamed him, even after I admitted my own fault in it. I pushed him away and now he was gone.

And I may never get the chance to make it right.

CHAPTER TEN

The crackling fire Nathaniel left going warmed me and Finn while we sat in silence and sipped some tea. It was late, all the patrons had gone to bed and most of the staff had long gone home. But Nathaniel's wife could be heard in the kitchen, cleaning up and preparing things for the next day. I took the last sip of my tea and set the mug down on the hard, wooden coffee table that divided the space between us. My nerves were catching up with me and it was getting harder to hide them.

"Dianna," Finn said quietly. "Ye needn't stress yerself. We'll find the wee ones."

I chewed at the inside of my cheek. "And what about Henry? The last time I saw him we…"

I shook my head and gripped my fingers together. I tore my gaze away from my friend and focused on the glowing embers beneath the flames in the fireplace. But Finn was too observant and too good of a friend. He could read me almost as well as anyone.

"We'll find the captain, and then ye can say all the things yer thinkin' in that pretty little head of yers."

With a shaky hand, I quickly wiped away the wetness that touched the underside of my eyes. I couldn't fall apart. Not now. Not yet. I nervously rubbed my hands over my thighs.

"I'll be puttin' out a call among the other sailors tomorrow," Finn said. "And I'll poke around the incoming travelers, see if they heard anything about the captain."

A single chuckle escaped my mouth in a huff of air. "You know. You don't have to call him captain. It's been almost five years."

"Aye," he replied solemnly. "But he'll always be my captain. He saved my life, many years ago, when he accepted me aboard The Devil's Heart. Henry is more than just a leader of some ship. He's family."

My brow pinched together with a thought. "You've never told me anything about your actual family. I mean, I obviously know you're from Scotland."

We both laughed.

"But that's it," I finished. "Who were you before you met Henry?"

Finn inhaled deep and long, his back straightening. Nostrils flared. "I was leaving behind a very dark and unwelcoming life. I snuck aboard the first ship I could find and made my way to England. It didn't take me long to cross paths with him. I was lookin' for a means to get as far away as possible, and he was recruitin' crew members for a ship. I ken how to navigate, the rest I picked up fast."

I ran tight fingers through my mess of hair and nodded. "Okay." I stood from the chair. "We should probably get some sleep. Lot's to do tomorrow."

Finn towered over me and clasp a hand on my shoulder. "Rest. Ye travelled a long way. Yer no good to anyone like this."

"No, I'm fine," I lied. "Just sleepy."

He cocked an eyebrow but said nothing. We both exited the common area and headed up to our rooms. He stood outside his door across the hall until I was secured behind mine. I threw a giant log on the fire and I crawled into the comfy bed, but my mind wouldn't let me fall asleep. My heart ached for Arthur and Audrey; I'd never been away from them. Not for one day in their short little lives. I'd kissed their heads and tucked them in each night for almost four years now and laying there, in an empty bed without Henry's arms around me, loneliness took hold of me.

The tears came hard and fast. My body shook with every failed attempt to stifle my cries and I curled into a tight ball under the blankets. With a shaky hand, I reached down to the floor next to the bed and pulled two tiny stuffed bunnies from my bag. They smelled of the kids and I pressed them both to my face as I inhaled the bittersweet aroma. A new wave of emotions crept in and wasted no time in forcing me further down into a pit of cold sorrow.

A soft knock rapped on the door and Finn opened it a crack to peek his head inside.

"Jesus, Mary n'Joseph," he whispered. "I can hear ye wailin' from across the hall."

I glanced up at him in the doorway with a tear-stained face and swollen eyes. "I'm sorry. I-I tried to hold it together," I said with a sob as he entered the room and shut the door. The bubbling howls just kept coming. "I... really did."

"Ye babies are missin," he said as he came around to the other side of the bed and crawled in behind me. "And so is the man ye love."

The giant jostled the bed as he made himself comfortable and hauled me backward toward him where my body shook in his arms. The oddly familiar embrace was comforting—reminding me of the nights I spent sharing a hammock with him—but failed to calm my violent weeping. He sighed at my back.

"Fall apart, Time Traveller. I got ye."

***

I set down a damp, wooden crate next to a large pile of them and the loud, hollow bellowed across The Queen's lower deck. Bouncing off the empty walls. This ship was once full of life and love. It was home to us as we sailed across the Atlantic on a suicide mission to find my sister. It's where Lottie grew up during the years her father, Red Jack Roberts, captained it. Before it became mine.

But it wasn't mine anymore.

Now she sat down by the docks like a lonely red beast. Moaning and creaking as the gentle waves slowly forced it to lap up against the buoys. It was a shame. Like seeing a wild, exotic animal locked in a small cage. She deserved the sea.

Finn and I had spent a better part of the day cleaning and reorganizing the neglected ship in anticipation that we might have to sail. My plan was to take one of the rowboats and paddle out a way during sunset. When the fledgling moonlight touched the sun's orange reflection on the waves.

"Dianna!" Finn's muffled voice sounded from above. "C'mere!"

I wiped my grimy hands on my slacks and climbed the short ladder to the upper deck where Finn waited with glee. He helped me up the last step and I stood to find we had company. The man, clad in dingy hunting gear, stood there patiently, his usual stoic self. His expression hardly wavering from staid. But I could see the hint of wonder and disbelief in his brown eyes.

"Gus!" I called out and took a few quick strides to him. He stuck out a hand to shake before I could wrap my arms around him. I accepted it with gusto. "It's good to see you."

He gave a single nod. "And I you." His brow pinched together. "What are you doing here?"

My chest heaved with a deep breath. "It's a long story, but I'm here to find my children. A siren took them and fled to the past. We had no choice but to come back."

"We?"

"Aye," Finn cut in, "The captain was with her, but they got separated. We dinnae know where the bugger is, but we'll find him."

I peered around his shoulder to find Lottie standing on the dock, arms crossed tightly, and her disgruntled gaze purposely averted from our tiny reunion.

"Didn't Lottie tell you all this?" I asked him.

Gus glanced over his shoulder and then back to us. "No. Charlotte's..." His expression darkened with impatience. "I heard from a local that a dark-haired woman was seen with Finnigan and that they were asking around about a man named Henry. Charlotte graced me with her knowledge of your return on our walk over here."

"Walk?" Lottie balked. "You dragged me here."

Gus exchanged a knowing glance with Finn.

"Regardless," Gus said to me. "We're here to help. Whatever you need." He half-turned and looked at his wife standing on the dock a few feet away. "*Both* of us."

To most, Gus's declaration would seem like nothing. But to me, someone who knew him, knew how very little of himself he shared, it meant so much. Lottie, on the other hand, I still couldn't wrap my head around her behaviour. My heart ached for the pain of her loss. But it's like she didn't even want me here.

"Thank you," I told him.

"What's your plan?" he asked.

"Finn and I are going to row out on the water once the sun begins to set," I explained. "I'm going to use my bizarre connection to the sea and ask for the siren, any siren, to appear."

He seemed to mull it over. "And you think the creature will help you find your children and Henry?"

I shrugged. "She took my kids as a way to force me to return to the past. I'm here and she's yet to show her face." I narrowed my eyes. "She *owes* me my kids."

Finn cleared his throat. "In the meantime, we're stocking the ship and gettin' her ready to sail. Just in case."

"Count me out," Lottie chimed in. "I'm not sailing anywhere."

Gus rolled his eyes and spun around. His wide hands grabbed her waist as if she were no more than a doll and forced her aboard. Lottie squirmed and slapped her husband's shoulder, but Gus was built like a small ox. There was no moving him.

Lottie's scrambling boots hit the deck and she stood frozen. Her face paled and my heart immediately clenched for her. I knew why she wouldn't come aboard. Not because of stubbornness. Not because of me.

Because this is where she lost her baby.

Her hard, watery gaze shot back and forth between the three of us. Traitors, in her mind, no doubt.

"I'll be down below," she said curtly and stormed off.

When she was out of sight, I turned to Gus.

"If Lottie's not comfortable -"

"She'll be fine," he replied quickly. "She needs to face this head-on, or she won't face it at all."

"Gus, if you'd both like to be alone to work through this, I would understand," I said. "You don't have to be here. Not after what you guys went through. Go, be with Lottie."

My old quartermaster stood a little taller and pride widened his shoulders. "My place is here, with you." His lips pressed together as he reconsidered. "And with her. She wants to be here, too. Trust me. Just give her time."

My chest filled with warmth at the comradery surrounding me. I'd made friends in this time who were closer to me than anyone I'd ever met. I cherished them like family because that's what they were. A family I've chosen for myself. And they've chosen me, for reasons I'll never understand but will forever be grateful for.

I smiled at Finn and Gus. "Even though the circumstances are awful, it feels good to have you guys with me. I just wish Benjamin were here, too."

They exchanged yet another curious glance and my mind immediately flew into a one-way trip to paranoia. Something was going on. Something Finn had yet to tell me. They were all separated when I arrived. For various reasons. And Lottie seemed to be working her way through all five stages of grief. All on her own. Stubborn woman.

Finn ruffled his long green coat and knocked away the dirt. "Dinnae worry, Ben will be back. He always comes back."

What was that supposed to mean?

"Plus," Finn added cheerily, "He's surely heard the whisperings of the likes of you hangin' around town. He'll be back. Trust me."

I chewed my lip in thought and then glanced out toward the horizon where the sun began to lower itself in the sky. I had other things to worry about besides what happened here in the last four and a half years.

"It's almost time," I said.

Finn nodded and went to hoist the rowboat down to the water. I unlatched the rolled-up rope ladder and flung it over the side. He descended to the boat first and then helped me when I got to the last step. We each took an oar and began paddling further out on the water. My time in the future had softened my muscles and I felt the strain on my arms almost right away. But adrenaline fuelled me now. I would soon be one step closer to finding my children.

I just hoped it worked.

Silence filled the little boat, aside from the sound of our oars cutting through the saltwater with each labored stroke. It had only been a few minutes when I heard someone shouting from behind us. A deep voice projecting through the air, crying my name.

We stopped rowing and I turned around to face the near-empty docks. It only took a fraction of a second to spot the Viking sized man waving his arms in the air. With his height and messy chestnut waves that hung from his head and face, Benjamin would stand out anywhere.

My heart kicked into overdrive and I waved to him. He ran his hands through his hair as he stumbled back a step, stunned. The backpack he wore slipped to the ground and he dove head-first into the water.

"Row back!" I said to Finn and stuck my paddle back in the water. My heart raced with every movement, eager to get to him. To the friend I left behind. Finn was right. He came back.

Benjamin reached the boat in no time and clung to the side to catch his breath. He took one look up at me waiting and hauled himself over the edge. He fell to the floor, still gasping for air but managed to laugh. Tears of wonder filled his eyes as he stared up at me. He hadn't changed at all. I reached out a hand to help him to his knees and, still, Benjamin towered over me. A sopping wet curtain of brown hair tickled my face as he leaned in, unblinking.

"You're here," he said.

I nodded, my grin barely contained.

His face lit up as the reality of the moment finally caught up with him and he grabbed my arms. He crushed me to him in a desperate hold and we both shook under the weight of his hysteric laughter. I let him hold me and took comfort in the familiar embrace. Years may have gone by, but my strange and unexplainable bond to this pirate hadn't altered one bit.

He pulled away and pressed his dripping forehead to mine as he lowered his voice. "You're... *here*."

"I am."

Finn coughed loudly. "I hate to break up this lovely reunion, but we got a siren to catch."

Benjamin froze and rocked back on his heels. "What are you talking about?"

"I'm here to get my kids back," I said. "The siren came to me in the future and demanded I come back. When I told her no, she took my children. I had no choice."

"And Henry?" he asked.

It felt as though I was going around in circles explaining myself to everyone. But this would be the last time if my plan worked.

"He came with me, but I ended up here without him. I'm hoping that perhaps the siren might be able to tell me where he landed."

He fell quiet as he thought about my words. "*How* did you get here?"

No one's asked me that one yet. "A pearl. The siren left me a wish pearl."

Finn moaned behind me and a wave of expressions washed over Benjamin's face. Disbelief and maybe a little guilt? No, something else was going on. But what?

He gazed out over the water and closed his eyes tightly. "You were going to touch the sun and moon on the water, weren't you?"

My brow pinched together. I didn't recall ever telling him about that little trick.

"How did you -"

"Give me the oar," Benjamin demanded. "I know what to do."

Without a word, I handed him my paddle and moved aside while he and Finn rowed us out a few more yards. The sun was low in the sky. Tones of purple and navy blended with the warm orange and I could see the silver glints of moonlight mixing with it on the waves.

But, before I could move, Benjamin flung down his oar and leaned over the edge next to me. A look of sheer determination on his face.

"Seneca Saye," he called. I peeked at Finn from the corner of my eye and he shrugged. "Seneca, I demand that you show yourself!"

"Ben, what are you doing?" I asked quietly.

He moved his hand rapidly in the water. "It's her

name."

"The siren?"

That same odd expression flickered across his face. "Yes. The siren. I've, uh, spoken to her before. She told me her name."

Finn leaned forward and jostled the boat, an incredulous look in his eye. "A creature of myth willingly gave you their *name*?"

Benjamin sighed. "Yeah, it's a long story." His hand splashed the water impatiently. "Seneca!"

Suddenly, the boat began to turn. Slowly, gently picking up speed. The sea around us twirled beneath the boat and I gripped the narrow edges as we flew in a circular motion. Wind and water whipped at our faces.

"What's happening?" I shouted.

"I dinnae know!" Finn bellowed back.

The waves slowly rose up around us as we circled the drain, and I realized then that we were being sucked down into a whirlpool. My eyes widened as I noticed the towering water collapsing from above and closing in the opening. Several tons of ocean water was hurdling down our way.

"Brace yourselves!" I yelled.

Ben covered me with his body and gripped the edge. I did my best to hold on to the side of the boat and Finn slid beneath the seat where he wrapped his arms tight around it. Freezing cold water smashed into us, pushing us further down into oblivion.

My fingernails bent under the stress of the failing

grip I held. Water pushed at me, knocking me to and fro inside the cage that Benjamin created with his body.

I held on for as long as I could until the pressure was too much and my lungs burned for air. My last breath squeezed from my chest and water filled my mouth before darkness closed in.

And I was gone.

CHAPTER ELEVEN

Blackness filled my vision and all sounds echoed off the empty walls of my mind. I was alone. Unmoving. I couldn't feel my body, yet, the strange sensation of something being pushed down my throat made me want to wake from the void.

My consciousness swam through the blindness, reaching for the surface of my mind. I realized then, the pushing in my throat was air, purposely being forced into me. Suddenly, I could feel pins and needles spreading across my chest, letting me know I was alive. My lungs expanded and deflated, again and again, until a rush of saltwater thrust itself from my body and my eyes flew open just in time to spew it on the ground.

"Christ!" Finn groaned and wiped at his mouth. He hunched over and his back heaved as he worked to catch his breath. "I thought ye were a goner."

My vision blurred around the edges, but I shakily sat up on the slick, flat rock I laid on and glanced around. Black stones surrounded us from all around and above, glassy with wetness. A cave? It was massive. A titanic cavern beneath the sea. Benjamin sat at my other side, a helpless and amazed expression plastered to his face. My chest felt tender.

"Did... did you do CPR on me?" I asked Finn.

He threw his hands up and let them fall to his thighs with a hard slap. "I dinnae ken what you call it. But I seen ye do it before. On Henry during that fire. I figured it be better than lettin' ye lay there like a dead fish."

I chuckled but winced when it hurt the bruise that was clearly forming under my clothes.

"Aye," he said, "Sorry. I dinnae ken how hard to push."

I nodded and tried to stand. Benjamin hopped to his feet and grabbed my arm to help me to mine.

"It's okay," I told Finn. "It's supposed to hurt. And you must have done something right." I gave a fragile smile. "I'm alive."

Benjamin kept close to my side. "And a good thing, too. Because I think this is some kind of siren den. You may just get that wish, after all, sweetness."

I took stock of our surroundings, aside from the never-ending wet rock that seemed to cover everything. Our rowboat lay in scraps and my stomach twisted in a hard knot at the sight of it. That could have been us.

Small pools of water sprinkled the vast cave floor and they glowed with some strange, illuminating blue light. In the distance, maybe a hundred feet deeper into the cave, a brighter light danced across the slick stone walls as it shone from around a sharp corner.

"I guess we head over there," I said and pointed.

"Lead the way, captain," Finn joked.

I rolled my eyes and began taking careful steps across the wet rocks, toward the light. My two companions followed close behind. As I passed one of the tide pools, I glanced inside to see how they were illuminated. Small white fish swam in circles. The light reflecting off their fledgling bodies. I leaned in closer, narrowing my eyes. They weren't fish at all.

They were sirens. Baby sirens.

Seven of them swam together in the little basin, their slender eel-like bodies pure white. Like a fresh pearl. Bone thin hands moved through the water. I reached inside to touch them, mesmerized by their beauty. But they became invisible the moment my skin touched them. My fingers passed right through one as if it were water.

"Dianna!" Benjamin hissed with concern. "For the love of God, don't mess with their young."

I stood up. "I wasn't going to hurt it." I beamed down at the little creatures. "They're just so cute."

He grumbled under his breath. "Yeah, but they grow up to be deadly things that will mess with your mind. Sirens are the scourge of the sea."

I guffawed. "Trust me, I know firsthand just how menacing these things can be."

His lips pressed together as he regarded me. I could tell there was something he wanted to say, but he grumbled and pointed ahead. "We should keep going."

"Aye," Finn added, "we're in the beast's lair now, don't stray."

We fell in a short line and walked carefully through the massive cavern; our path highlighted by the tiny pools of offspring. The sudden soft sound of music lured us closer. When we approached the back, where it drastically turned a corner to the light, I quickened my pace. My children could very well be around that corner. My heart pounded hard inside my chest, pushing blood hot and fast through my veins. My fingers gripped the rock that jutted out from the turn and I peered around. Ben was right. This was some sort of siren's lair.

Half a dozen of them lounged across rock beds, surrounded by pools of water, twisting their seaweed hair into intricate braids and bathing in the very light that seemed to emanate from their pearl-like bodies. The sound, the music that carried through the air like mist, it came from them, too.

But their mouths never opened.

One of the stunning beasts froze in place as her face titled toward the dripping ceiling and she sniffed the air. In a split second, her head whipped in our direction, where our faces poked out from behind the stone wall. The siren's clear eyes filled with an inky substance and turned to two black almond-shaped globes on her face. A shrill, high-pitched screech pierced the air and scratched against the cavern walls before bouncing back to our ears. The sound was like jagged glass to my eardrums and only magnified as her sisters became alerted and joined in. The three of us covered the sides of our head and fell in a crouching ball as the siren's wail beat down on us.

"Enough!" a terrifying, but musical voice carried over the commotion.

The shrieking came to a halt, but the remnants still echoed in my ears as I stood to find a siren rising from the water, one that I recognized. Her green, iridescent scales were covered in all sorts of treasures from the sea; shells, rocks, and a crown made of broken coral. She grinned widely, showing a mouth full of terrifying white spikes.

This was the same siren from Shellbed Isle. I'd recognize the beautiful beast anywhere.

"Dianna Cobham," she said with a wet purr. "I didn't expect to see you here again. In *this* time. Why do you call to my sister from above?"

Benjamin stepped forward. "Where is Seneca Saye?"

The coven of sirens let out a resounding hiss and their queen narrowed her dark eyes.

"You dare speak my sister's name!" She emerged further out of the water and her long tail morphed into a set of legs as she stepped onto the cave floor on which we stood.

"She willingly gave it to me," he defended. "I would never abuse the right to use it."

"You do not possess the right to use it at all." She clicked her teeth together. "Yet, here you are. Demanding her presence."

It was my turn now. "He was only asking her to show because she stole my children. We're here to ask for them back."

She regarded me curiously, her bulbous, alien-like eyes blinking like a lizard's as a cloudy film flashed over them from the sides. "I'm aware of what my sister's been up to." Her gaze flickered to Ben and she grinned wildly. "For some time now."

"Then you know that she tricked me into coming back here," I said. "She kidnapped my children and forced me to use a pearl. This is all her doing."

"Yes, Seneca has always been a bit troublesome," the siren queen admitted. "It's why I've banished her to the realm of Faerie for angering the Keepers. She cannot be summoned in this human realm."

Finn let out a gutsy moan and began muttering Scottish curse words that may as well have been Chinese for all I could understand.

"Keepers?" Ben asked in a whisper.

My throat tightened. "But where are my *kids*?"

"I was not aware she took your children, Dianna Cobham. That much I swear. If Seneca truly possesses them still, then they will be with her in Faerie."

"Bring me there!" I insisted as I fought back anger.

The siren's head tilted to the side. "You hold no sway over me. You cannot command me to do anything."

"Please," I begged. "I'm not commanding anything. I just..." my voice broke with bubbling sobs. "I just want my children back. Take me to Faerie."

Her long, crooked finger clawed at the air between us. "You travel between the threads of time as if the consequences mean nothing to you. You bend the laws of everything that holds our world together, just to suit your own selfish needs. *Selfish.* You're no better than your thief of a mother. All you Cobham women are just alike."

I shook my head and looked to Finn in confusion. He just looked at me in stunned helplessness.

"I'm sorry," I said sincerely. "I don't know what you're talking about."

The creature's toothy grin widened even further, and her head cocked from side to side and she neared me. I could smell the sea wafting from her.

"You do not know." She seemed to take delight in this. "Your mother dearest stole the very pearl that sent her to the future so many years ago. It's what started all of this. Your birth, your existence, and the series of events that have led you to this very moment." Her pointed chin tipped upwards. "Constance Cobham disrupted the sanctity of time and was punished accordingly. And here you are, her own daughter, making the same mistakes."

I shook my head to make sense of everything she said. My mouth gaped as I searched for a response. "How was she punished?"

Then it hit me like a ton of bricks. My sister.

My face twisted in disgust. "You purposely gave her a siren child with no soul, didn't you? Maria didn't change after Mom failed to get back the siren's heart. She was already damned, wasn't she? *That* was my mom's punishment?"

"Your mother tried to find The Black Soul?" Benjamin asked me in disbelief.

"Yes," I told him. "Years ago. After she was ripped from me when I was a child. I thought she drowned. Turns out, the witches who raised her pulled her back through time. And, when her grief over losing me consumed her, she begged the sirens for help. She asked for a baby and they gave her Maria Cobham."

"Christ," Finn blew out in a huff.

I turned my gaze back to the siren queen and shot her a piercing look. "But that wasn't enough for you, was it? You had to send her on a wild goose chase, a mission you knew she'd fail, so she'd think that it was *her* fault that Maria was cursed."

"But you did it," Benjamin reminded me. "You

found my ship. *You* returned the heart. It wasn't an impossible mission."

"And Dianna was rewarded greatly," the siren chimed in.

I nodded in understanding as all the jumbled pieces of my existence finally began to make sense. "The bracelet of pearls."

"You succeeded where your mother could not," the sea creature spoke. "We honor our promises just as true as we uphold our duty to protect the sanctity of time in union with The Keepers. You had everything you wanted in the future, even a man who belonged to the past. We allowed it to happen. Yet, here you are, wasting the gifts you've been so graciously given and making demands you have no right to. Have you not learned your lesson, Dianna Cobham?"

I took a step closer. "I did nothing! Your deranged sister did this! *All* of this."

She inhaled deeply through her nose, her nostrils flaring like the gills of a fish. "Be that as it may, I can grant you the ability to travel to our sacred realm of Faerie to retrieve your children." She bent down and reached into the glowing water by her side and scooped out a single black pearl. "A wish for an exchange."

I glanced between my two friends and then eyed her curiously. "Exchange of what?"

She grinned madly and inched closer, offering the pearl in the palm of her scaly hand. "Your soul."

"Absolutely not!" Benjamin spat and stuck his

arm out across my body. "Dianna shouldn't have to sacrifice anything for this. She did nothing wrong."

Her head whipped in Ben's direction. "Do you offer your soul in place of hers, then?"

Without missing a beat, he replied, "Yes. Take mine."

"Benjamin!" I cried and gripped his arm. "No, you can't do that. Not after everything we did to get it back. You spent a lifetime without one, tethered to that damn ship."

"Aye," Finn agreed. "Lad, dinnae give up what Dianna worked so hard give ye. Dinnae let her sacrifices be in vain."

Pain drenched his expression. "But what if it kills her?"

I turned to the beast. "It won't. Right?"

The siren chuckled quietly under her breath as she watched us and gave me a single nod. It sickened me how much delight these beings really took in the misery of humans.

My fists tightened at my sides. "Deal. Take my soul and give me the wish pearl. But you allow me and my two friends to leave unharmed."

She advanced slowly, stepping across the wet rocks on which we all stood. Her sisters sat quietly in the background, watching in anticipation. The siren stopped at my feet and the stench of old seaweed and fish filled my nose. Her throat made a weird clicking sound as she inhaled the surrounding air.

I flinched when her mouth widened into a

menacing grin, flashing those jagged teeth just inches from my face. "Done."

"Dianna," Benjamin begged me in a helpless whisper. For such a large and rugged man, he was nothing but soft on the inside. Ruled by his bleeding heart. I pursed my lips and squeezed his hand. "Don't. You don't have to do this."

"These are my children, Ben."

I let go of his hand and stepped away. I motioned with my head for Finn to keep him back and the Scottish giant stood closer to him, ready to grab Ben if need be.

"I'm ready," I told the siren queen.

I inhaled deeply, readying myself for what was to come, but the sea creature spared no time. Her long arm shot out and her hand struck my chest like a hammer. The painful hit knocked me backward, but I didn't fall to the ground. My body suspended in the air as she circled around it, dragging her slimy seaweed hair behind her.

I felt my body closing in on itself as magic sucked my soul right through the pores of my skin. Boiling my blood and crushing my lungs. I choked for air, but it was no use. She was wringing me out like a damp sponge, squeezing every last drop of my soul. From the corner of my eye, I could see Benjamin yelling my name, but the sound of his voice failed to reach my ears. Finn struggled to hold him back. A guttural scream of agony forced itself from deep inside, allowing the last tendril of myself to escape.

And just as quickly as it began, the pain came to a screeching halt and I fell to the ground with a hefty thump. I rolled to my side and gasped for air as Ben and Finn ran to me.

"Note to self," I said to them and wheezed, "Having a soul extracted hurts like hell."

"Aye, Time Traveller," Finn groaned as he helped me stand. "Henry will have my head if I don't keep ye in one piece."

I stumbled as I let the full weight of me rest on my feet and Benjamin caught me. His strong arm slid under mine and around my back, taking all my weight, and the three of us regarded the siren who stood by, unmoving and pleased with herself.

"What will happen to me now?" I asked her.

Her shoulders shrugged carelessly. "Nothing. You are rendered immortal, but not invincible. Without a soul you will not age, will not die by the hands of time. Be warned, although that may seem like a gift, it is not."

I felt Ben tense at my side.

I nodded. "I know."

The siren held out the pearl. "But this is. Use it wisely. You only get one chance."

I picked the black bead from her palm and secured it in my jacket pocket.

"How do we get out of here?" Benjamin asked the creature. "You destroyed our boat." He guffawed. "Not that it would help all the way down here, anyway."

"Head to the mouth of the cavern," she told us.

"The sea will guide you to the surface."

I nodded and began to turn.

"Before you go." The words slipped off her slimy tongue like poison. "I have something for you to consider."

We stood and watched as the sea queen walked toward her sisters and clapped her hands together. Without a word, they all slid off the rocks they laid on and revealed a large stone shaped like a jagged box the size of a coffin.

"Open," she ordered.

Their long white arms hauled on the slab of stone that served as a lid of some kind and pushed it aside. A loud, muffled scream boomed from inside as they all reached in and pulled out a man. His panicked eyes immediately fled to mine and widened.

"Henry!" I screeched as I slipped away from Benjamin's hold and ran to him. But the siren queen flung out her arm stopped me in my tracks.

"Your beloved has been safe with us this entire time," she said. "And he'll remain here if you do not choose wisely."

"*What*?" I said with a gasp.

Tears swelled in my eyes, matched by Henry's as he stared helplessly at me. His mouth gagged with a fistful of dried kelp. Rage vibrated all around him, but he was in rough shape. Paled skin, soaking wet clothes, bloodied wounds on his face.

"It doesn't look like he's been safe here," I added. "Release him right now."

The siren's brow arched in my direction. "Care to make that a wish?"

My stomach turned and my throat tightened. "No, y-you can't…" I backed away slowly, with no soul to garner my emotions, they ran wild in my heart. The sudden pain of the impossible situation seared my insides and my gut clenched tightly as I let out a fierce cry. "No! You can't do this. You can't make me choose! That's not fair!"

"There's no place for fairness in this life, Dianna Cobham. You above all should understand this." The siren stood taller, smug with her cleverness. "Choose now. Save your husband or enter Faerie to save your children. You only get a single wish."

I shook my head, refusing to believe this was the choice I truly had. I'd planned on asking the sirens for help in finding Henry, to see if they knew of his whereabouts. Where he fell in time. Apparently, he'd been here the whole time, a victim to the torturous clutches of these insidious creatures.

I stared deep into his eyes from across the way and he feverishly shook his head. Henry spat a few times until the kelp fell from his mouth.

"Don't!" he called to me; his hands secured behind his back. "Dianna! Wish for the children! Save Arthur and Audrey. Leave me here."

Snotty sobs emerged from my face and my shoulders slumped under the impossible weight of everything. "I can't. I don't know how to make this right."

"Dianna," he said, attempting to smooth out the

tremble in his voice.

"I can't live without you," I cried quietly, tears spilling down my face. "Don't ask me to do this."

"I'm not," he replied. "I'm asking you to save them. It's what we came back for." My cries pained him to witness and he cringed. I knew his arms ached to hold me as much as mine did for him because his agony mirrored my own.

I startled as Finn's gentle hand pressed against my shoulder and his face leaned into my ear, his usually loud voice lowered to a barely audible whisper. "Dinnae worry about the kids, lass. I ken a way to Faerie. I swear it. Save the captain. I'll get ye where ye need to go."

My eyes searched his for any sign of uncertainty, but I was only met with a stone-cold look of certitude.

"Are you sure?" I whispered. He nodded.

My chest lightened under the release of stress and my heart fluttered with possibility. I could save Henry and find the kids. The sirens knew I'd choose my children over him. Expected it, in fact. I could tell from the way they waited, an expression of sheer hunger on their eerie faces. A hunger for my misery.

I grinned and reached into my pocket for the pearl before holding it over the water. Henry's eyes bulged and he struggled against the restraints behind his back.

"Dianna! No!"

He would understand later when I explained

everything. But, for now, I had to let him believe I was choosing him. I had to outsmart these creatures of the sea, these beasts who continued to taunt my lineage. The pearl dropped into the pool of water and began to disintegrate.

The siren queen's head cocked back and forth in disbelief and she hissed.

"I wish for you to set Henry free and allow him to return to me unharmed."

Her sisters joined her, and their ear-piercing shrieks filled the cave once again. Clearly, they weren't used to being bested.

"A deal is a deal," I reminded the queen and the wailing stopped. "Give me my husband."

She clenched her fists. "Very well."

The siren sisters cut the ties from behind his back and Henry weakly climbed out of the stone coffin before running through the shallow narrow of water that separated us. My breathing quickened as I ran to him and we collided. My hands mauled his skin, taking note of every scratch and bruise, shaking as I held his face and kissed him.

But he pushed me away.

Shocked, I looked up at him to find nothing but malice waiting for me.

"Why did you do that?" he bellowed.

I cowered inwardly. "Henry -"

Our attention immediately diverted to the sudden movement of the sirens from behind. They'd all dove into the water and disappeared without a trace. Their queen glared at all of us before following her sisters and we were soon left alone in the hollow, enchanting cavern.

Water lapped and my feet and filled the gouges in the rocks around us. I noticed then, the water level in the pools, it was rising.

And fast.

"We need to get out of here," Benjamin warned us.

The four of us turned and ran back in the direction I'd come with my two friends, our boots slipping with every other step as the water level continued to rapidly rise. It was already at our knees when we reached the mouth of the cave, the siren's den far behind us and out of sight. The vast and darkened ocean waited just on the other side. A strange, invisible force held it back from the cave opening, like a wall, preventing it from pouring in and filling the pocket of space we stood in.

"I think we have to swim," I told them.

Finn rubbed his hands over his face. "Christ, we have no idea how far up the surface is. We could drown."

"Well, we're going to drown in here in mere minutes," Benjamin pointed out and noted the water level now at our waists.

My chest heaved in anticipation. We didn't have time to debate this. We had seconds before this cave would fill with water and we'd have no choice but to swim. Without a second thought or another word, I turned and dove through the wall of water and exited the cavern.

Immediately, the stark cold of the untouched ocean depths shocked my body, but I swam as hard as I could, kicking my feet and reaching for the surface. I could see it, in the distance. The misty glow of moonlight covering it, showing us the way.

Henry was by my side and grabbed my hand. Together we swam to the surface faster and our two comrades followed close behind. It seemed like forever had slowly ticked by, every stroke more labored than the last. My lungs strained and burned with a lack of oxygen and my limbs began to go numb.

Still, I swam.

Finally, just when I was ready to accept that we'd never make it, when the air in my lungs had long died, we broke the surface. The four of us bobbed in place, desperately gasping for breath. I spotted The Queen not far in the distance. Close enough to catch the waving arms of Gus on deck. Still shook from the ordeal, we tiredly swam toward the ship and hauled ourselves up the rope ladder that Gus lowered. One by one, we all collapsed on deck in a heap of stress and seawater while Gus ran off to fetch some blankets.

I reached for Henry, but he shrunk away.

"I can't believe you," he spat between heavy panting.

"Henry, you don't understand," I pleaded. "Finn knows a way to Faerie. He can help us find the kids. I *had* to save you." It killed me that he refused my touch.

"Dianna, you offered your soul as if it means *nothing*!"

I cowered away.

He twisted his neck and peered at Finn as his blonde hair fell down around his face. "It's good to see you old friend. But is that true? Can you get us to Faerie?"

Finn's beady eyes shot back and forth between Henry and I and he groaned nervously. "Aye, I ken a way. I grew up listenin' to the tales of the land of Fae. I reckon I can find the door."

Henry turned and glared at me.

My throat tightened. "Wait. Do you mean..." I took a few deep breaths. "Finn, you grew up in Scotland. Are you saying the hidden passage to Faerie is in *Scotland*?"

Benjamin closed his eyes and sighed. "Oh, Finn..."

"What was I supposed to *do*?" he defended himself. "The captain was bound by sirens and the lass was fallin' apart. *No* one should be faced with a choice like that."

I fought to control my breathing, but the short, quickened gasps threatened my oxygen supply. My mind spun from the trauma of everything that just happened. Thinking back, it all seemed like a blur, it happened so fast. But now, here on the ship and safe, I never felt more vulnerable.

Henry hauled himself to his feet and glared down at me with eyes brimming with emotions. "You made the wrong choice. You put our children's lives further at risk, all on the slim chance of a fickle fairy tale and a three-month voyage at sea."

"Hey, she's trying her best," Benjamin jumped in. "What would *you* have done?"

Henry spun around and advanced on Ben. "I would have chosen my kids. Without a second thought."

Ouch. I recoiled instantly, his words cutting deep into my heart. Henry was my everything, my other half, my soul mate. But he was right. About it all. I should have chosen Arthur and Audrey over Henry. Now I may never get them back.

What have I done?

CHAPTER TWELVE

Four sets of eyes diverted from meeting one another's gaze as the five of us sat around the table in the mess hall aboard The Queen. I couldn't help but think of the hostilities in this one room, how everyone was mad at someone for reasons of their own. Henry could hardly stand to look at me. He was furious, and I didn't blame him. Not anymore. I shouldn't have to begin with. Ben was off in his own mind, working through lord knows what. And Lottie harbored an anger for the whole world, refusing to let it go.

Finally, Finn slammed his two fists on the table, causing the few bottles of spices and sauces to topple over. "That's enough," he said sternly but hinted with worry. "I'm sorry for what I did, I was just tryin' to help. Like it or not, we're goin' to Scotland. It's all we've got." His eyes landed on each one of us as he peered around the table. "The question is, who will captain the voyage?"

My stomach rolled. The thought of a few months at sea delighted me in ways I'd long forgotten. But being away from my children for another three whole months made me want to die.

I cleared my dry throat. "Gus. I gave the ship to Gus. He should captain the trip." I looked at my old quartermaster. "If you'll brave the journey. No one should be here if they don't want to be."

He sighed quietly; his expression unwavering. "I'm with you every step of the way. But the ship doesn't belong to me. It's yours, fair and square. I was simply taking care of her in your absence. These are your children, your ship. You should captain the voyage."

I shook my head. "No. I'm not fit to lead you guys. Not after all this time, not after…everything. I just don't have it in me to do it again." I sucked in a deep breath and dared shoot a sideways glance at my brooding husband who sat with his chair half-turned away from the table. "Henry should do it."

No one disagreed.

After a moment, Henry stood from his chair and frowned at the floor. Slipping back into the role of captain wasn't something he wanted, either. I knew that. But he was a much better fit than me. I didn't trust myself to make the right decisions when they mattered most.

He regarded the table of friends and crew. "Very well. It's truly wonderful to see you all, I just wish it were under better circumstances." He turned to leave but stopped and glanced over his shoulder with a darkened gaze. "We leave for Scotland in one day's time. You all know what to do. Prepare the ship."

Everyone scattered, eager to jump into their tasks. I bolted up and followed my husband out of the mess hall and down through the empty corridors of the ship. Moonlight filtered in through the portholes, creating a pattern of shadows as we walked. He knew I was behind him but refused to turn and face me. Still, I followed.

"Can't you just talk to me?" I called to his back.

He came to a screeching halt and spun around, the long flaps of his black leather coat twirling dramatically. His darkened stare glistened in the silver light he stood in.

"You sold your damn *soul*." His lip trembled. "What do you want me to say, Dianna?"

My shoulders slumped. "I don't know! Anything? What happened with the sirens before we came?" I took a step closer and he backed away. "How are we supposed to get through this if you won't even *touch* me?"

I saw his fists clenching at his sides as his gaze fell to the floor in thought.

"Take stock of the kitchen," he spoke through his teeth. "See what we need for the journey."

I bit my tongue. There was so much I wanted to say, so much we need to air out. But Henry wasn't ready, that much I could see. The poor man had been through so much in his life, it's a wonder the trauma of all he's faced hasn't completely broken him. I loved him with all my heart, but his was a dark one not so easily tamed. My husband was often fuelled by his ability to lock away his emotions. And, for now, I'd let him. He needed it.

I took in a shaky breath as I squashed down my pride and arched a brow. "Very well, *Captain*."

***

The next morning, I was down on my hands and knees, rooting through the shelves and cupboards in the severely neglected kitchen. Finn said they came back from England a short time ago, but it seemed as though the kitchen hadn't been looked after for months.

Bins of dried, half-rotten produce needed to be thrown out and refilled before we set sail. Bags of flour had gotten wet and were no good. Dirty, food crusted dishes lay in heaps across the counter. I wasn't sure if they could even be saved.

What the hell happened here?

I pushed myself to my feet and my elbow knocked a pot that had been teetering on the edge of the counter. It crashed to the floor with a loud smashing sound.

"Damn it," I muttered and bent down to fetch it.

"Need a hand?" Finn asked as he entered the room.

My cheeks immediately ran hot and I tossed the pot in the pile of dirty dishes. "No, I'm fine."

"Are ye alright?"

I didn't answer.

He groaned. "Do ye want to talk about it?"

I still didn't answer.

Finn let out a raspy sigh and leaned against the wall. "Yer mad at me."

I just kept shuffling garbage around the kitchen.

He waited a moment before shoving off the wall. "Fine then. I'll leave ye be."

I wanted to talk to him. I needed my friend, now more than ever. But I was lost in a cloud of my own torment and guilt as I tried to fight through the mess I created. He stormed out of the kitchen, letting the swinging door slam against the wall.

This was going to be a rough trip.

***

After a tiresome day of cleaning and stocking The Queen of everything we could possibly need for a long trip at sea, I sat on the edge of my bed and let it all sink in. Hardly anyone spoke a single word to me the entire day as we came and went, hauling boxes, bags, and crates of goods. Ben spent the day up in the masts, mending sails and securing all the ropes. He was ecstatic to see me at first; when he jumped off the dock and swam to me. But ever since our time down in the siren's den, he'd barely even looked in my direction.

I felt utterly alone.

I couldn't cry, not here in this tiny cabin room. Everyone would hear. It was barely large enough to fit the bed and a couple of chests. A single candle burned on the nightstand as my legs dangled off the side of the hay stuffed mattress, my fingers twisting together in a nervous knot. How could I possibly sleep knowing everything that lay ahead in the morning?

A single, gentle knock at the door yanked me out of my pit of despair.

"Come in," I said, expecting Finn to come and attempt amends again, but it was Henry who opened the door and peered inside. I swallowed nervously. "Hello."

"May I come in?"

I nodded, my heart fluttering to life. Henry wanted to talk to me.

He entered and shut the door behind him before easing himself down on the bed next to me, careful to leave a few inches between us. Baby steps. Henry wasn't the type to be pushed.

He moaned a sigh and combed his hands through his hair as he leaned forward. "Can I stay with you tonight?"

The flutters in my chest quickened and my heart raced in its cage. "Y-yes, of course." I swallowed against the tightness in my throat. It killed me the night before, sleeping alone again knowing he was just in the next room. "Are you -"

Without looking, Henry held up a hand. "Don't. Not yet. I'm still furious with you, with myself." He groaned and sat up straight, finally looking at me. The pain in those black eyes struck me hard. "But I can't stand to spend another night without you. Not after being with the sirens, not after *everything*. We should be together, even in times of anger."

Hot tears streamed down my face, seeping in between my pursed lips. "Henry, I'm sorry. You have no -"

"Dianna, I'm tired. *So* tired," he cut in impatiently. "I don't want to speak; I don't want to face anything right now. I only want to fall asleep holding you in my arms and forget about who's mad at whom just for one night." He braved a glance up at me from under the curtain of messy yellow waves that half-covered his face. "Can we do that?"

Again, I could only afford a nod. The words and emotions building inside were ready to explode and I didn't think he was ready for me to unleash it. I wanted Henry to take me in his arms and demand my mouth, to remind me of how it feels to be loved by him. It'd only been days since my lips touched his but it may as well have been a lifetime for the distance I felt between us. If all he wanted to sleep by my side, I would take it. I would take any part of him I could get.

Slowly, I removed my jacket and slipped out of

my dingy clothes. I desperately needed a bath, but it would have to wait. Henry did the same, slugging out of his heavy coat and hung all our clothes from the hooks at the back of the door.

I slid under the quilt and he crawled in behind me, closest to the wall. My insides warmed immediately at his touch as Henry's long arm wrapped around my waist and held my back tight to his chest. He was sleeping in minutes, the soft sound of his purr-like snores filling the room and soothing my frazzled nerves.

Soon, my breathing fell in sync with his, but my heart refused to quit. I laid awake, in Henry's sleeping arms, as my mind obsessed over everything that lay ahead. We were banking a lot on the slim chance that Finn could find the gateway to Faerie. We could waste three months at sea only to discover there was no door. I kept circling around to a single thought. One question. Did I make the right decision?

Again, only one solution arose in my mind; what choice did I have?

∗∗∗

It'd been a few days now and The Queen smoothed along the West Coast of Newfoundland, heading North so we could hug the tip of the peninsula as we emerged into the Labrador Sea. After that, we'd be surrounded by never-ending horizons until we crossed the Atlantic and docked in Scotland.

I busied about the kitchen, reorganizing it to my liking. I assumed the role of the ship's cook once again, being the best candidate, but also welcoming the distraction from all the tension aboard. Everyone was still so full of silent anger. Gus and Lottie, who hardly exchanged a word, with each other or anyone else. Lottie had yet to even come up on deck.

Henry made small advances by sleeping in my bed each night, but he made sure to slip out in the morning before I awoke. Ben was nowhere to be found, spending most of his time in his cabin or up in the crow's nest. I obsessed over his pattern of actions. How he was ecstatic to discover I'd come back, but completely shut me out after we saved Henry. Was he uncomfortable around us? It couldn't be. I hated to think that he still had feelings for me after all these years. But what other reason could there be for his odd behaviour?

The door swung open and I looked up from the bowl of dough I mixed and heaved a sigh. Then there was Finn. He stood there in the doorway and waited hopefully. I rolled my eyes and pointed at a tray on the farthest counter.

"There are rosemary buns over there."

He took a bun and groaned loudly as he slumped down in a wooden chair. It buckled under his weight. "Dianna, if ye don't soon forgive me, I'll lose me Jesus mind." He lobbed off a chunk of the bread and stuffed it to the side of his bearded mouth. "I was only doing what I thought to be right. I couldn't very well leave the captain there with the wretched beasts."

I swam through my thoughts. "I know, Finn." He brightened. "I know you didn't mean any harm. But look where it got us. We're embarking on another flimsy mission in the hopes you can find a mythical door."

He sat up straight. "I can. I *will* find it. I swear." His head cocked to the side and his eyes filled with tears. "Christ, if I were a Viking, I'd whisk us away in the blink of an eye but I cannae. I'm sorry. Just please forgive me for the love' a God, Dianna. I cannae *stand* it."

I stopped kneading the dough and my face twisted in confusion. "Viking?"

He rolled his eyes and waved it off. "Ahh, the buggers were always leavin' portals wherever their boats landed. Wherever they conquered or settled."

My pulse quickened. "Portals?"

He muttered something Gaelic under his breath. "Aye, it's how the savages moved around. Dinnae ye ken that in the future? In yer history books?"

I laughed. "Viking portals? No, can't say I learned anything about that in high school." I removed my hands from the bowl and wiped the sticky bits of dough on my apron. "Finn, are you certain about this?"

He seemed confused and shrugged. "Aye. I seen them with me own eyes as a wee lad."

I untied my apron and tossed in on the counter. "This would have been extremely helpful to know when we first sailed to England."

He shook his head. "Nae, the Vikings never reached the shores of Newfoundland. It wasn't an option. There be no portals here."

I raced across the room and wrapped my arms around my friend with glee. He nestled his face in my hair and chuckled as he slung both arms around my back.

"Not that I'm not grateful for the embrace, lass, but care to let me in on whatever it is yer thinkin'?"

I pulled away and stood back, a smile plastered across my face. "I guess you guys don't know yet, but there's a Viking settlement on the Northern Peninsula." Finn's face brightened and he slowly stood up. "It's found in my time and partially uncovered. It's, like, a thousand years old. So, even here, it would be well over seven hundred years ago. Way before the first settlers came."

"Where?" His brows raised in anticipation. "We may never find it. The Northern Peninsula is vast and untouched."

I grinned. "The settlement is literally right at the very tip. It couldn't be easier to find."

He rubbed his fingers over his beard as he thought. "We could make it in less than two days. Christ, we're nearly there." He nodded slowly to himself as the thoughts seemed to be reforming in his mind. "And ye sure of this?"

I smiled. "Absolutely. It's huge. People come from

all over the world to see it."

"Then there's surely a portal there," he replied happily and tore off another bite of the bun with his teeth. "Let's go tell the others."

I followed him out of the kitchen and across the ship before we headed up on deck. The tingly feeling of hope-filled my chest. Finally, a break. A glimmer of promise on our side.

CHAPTER THIRTEEN

My life felt as if it were going in fast forward and slow motion all at once. It didn't take long for the crew the readjust plans and steer us back toward land. To the Northern Peninsula of Newfoundland. We'd make landfall by morning and it only took two days to get where we were now. How fast things move when there's hope. *So* fast. Yet, my progress with Henry was slow.

Painfully slow.

I sat across the table from him on the mess deck. No one else had arrived for lunch yet. I spent all morning making fish stew and fresh buns but finished too soon. Henry was the first to show and now we just sat there. Waiting. For what, exactly, I had no idea. Waiting for things to change? Waiting for something to click and put the pieces of us back together again?

We spent nights cradled together in bed. Although he was steadfast in his determination to avoid going any further than a single arm draped over my waist, it gave me a sliver of hope. That, one day, Henry wouldn't be mad at me. And I think it was his way of letting me know I was right; he just needed time.

Still, I wished he talked to me.

We'd been sitting at the table for fifteen minutes and the only words exchanged were about what I made for lunch. Now we sat there in silence.

Waiting.

We were about to embark on a journey that would take us to a part of Newfoundland that hadn't been touched in over seven hundred years. So we could search for ancient Viking stones and use them as a portal to travel to Scotland and find a way into the realm of Faerie.

It sounded like a load of crazy. The more I thought it over, the less it made sense to me. The enormity of it all. How a series of events such as the last five years could actually happen. To me, no less. One person who gets to experience the throes of piracy and ocean sorcery. Of time travel and mythical beasts. It was almost too much for one person to take.

Finally, I'd had enough. I leaned back in the chair in a huff.

I needed my husband. My best friend. My soul mate.

Not this mute of a giant blonde pirate. This ancient persona that Henry so easily slipped back into. Devil Eyed Barrett. The brooding tortured young captain and his blind march through life.

I reached across the table to take his hand in mine, to remind him of what it feels like to touch me outside of sleep. I'd come accustomed to Henry's hands on my body; a gentle caress, a long embrace, my hand in his. He would always find ways to touch me, to let me know he loved me. And I missed it with every fiber of my body.

I rested my hand over his for a moment, smiling at his weary face. Willing him to smile along with me. To give me another sliver of hope. But he flinched away and slipped his hand under the table. My heart deflated in my chest and my stomach tightened. I tried not to cry as Henry stood up from the bench.

"I'll just serve myself a bowl and be on my way."

I shot up. The tears right there, pushing to get out. "You can't stay mad at me forever."

Henry spun around and stared intently. "You don't have the right to decide when I should stop feeling angry. Besides..." he guffawed and shook his head. "It's not anger I'm feeling. It's *grief*."

I hung my head in shame as a single tear streamed down my cheek. "The kids. I know. The grief takes my breath away at times."

Henry was in front of me in seconds by a single lunge. "Then why didn't you *come* to me? Why did you push me away with blame?" His pit-less eyes glossed over. "Our children are lost. When we needed each other the most, you distanced yourself the furthest and found comfort in others. In a man who's consumed by his unrequited love for you."

I recoiled just as the sound of arriving footsteps sounded from behind.

I shook my head. "It's not like that with me and Ben. He's...I just can't explain it. I feel as though we were *meant* to know one another. But not in the way you think." I swallowed hard and braved half a step closer. "Not like you and me."

Henry's glassy gaze stared deep into mine and I wished more than ever that I could, just in that moment, read his mind. His torn expression averted over my shoulder, to the people who'd approached. I stole a glance in the same direction to find Gus and Lottie who stood awkwardly in the entrance to the mess deck.

Henry sighed and looked pointedly at Gus. "What do *you* think?"

Gus cleared his throat and exchanged an awkward glance with his wife. She rolled her eyes and tilted her impatient face at me. Regardless of what she was battling inside, I could always count on Lottie to tell it to me straight.

"He's always cared for you, Dianna," she said. "That's no secret. You know that yourself."

"But it's been years," I replied, dumbfounded.

Lottie chortled. "Do you think a few years would change the way you feel about Henry?"

I didn't need to look at him. I knew he was watching for my reaction.

My voice barely came out a loud whisper. "Nothing could ever change that."

Gus grumbled under his breath and crossed his arms. "Ben's been pining for you since day one. He would have done anything to get you back."

My breath hitched as the sudden realization, the missing piece of the puzzle smacked me in the chest and my heart gave one hard thump. A chilly sweat broke out across my skin.

Benjamin.

He was in love with me. He...knew the siren's name, knew how to summon her.

I yanked at the apron knot around my back and ripped the apron off before whipping it on the table. A frustrated groan erupted from within.

"That son of a bitch!"

I stormed off through the tables and over to the ladder hatch that brought me to the upper deck. Henry, Lottie, and Gus followed as I scanned all around for Ben. I found him in a corner, winding thick rope into loops. When he caught my gaze as I stormed across the wooden floor he smiled, but it quickly wiped away when he saw the look of fury in my eyes.

I hauled back and slapped his bearded face. I knew my lean arms could hardly put a dent in Benjamin's thick exterior, but I may as well have hit him with a sledgehammer for how much pain I found in his expression.

I couldn't care about that.

I squashed down my emotions and looked him sternly in the face, my finger jabbing his hard chest. "Was it you?"

Finn appeared and the crew had encroached together as they stood by in confused anticipation. Ben didn't say anything, just pleaded with his warm, brown eyes. Begged me to stop. But it only angered me further. How dare he stand there, confronted with what he'd done, and make me feel bad about it.

"Tell me!" I screamed at him. "You did it, didn't you? You wished for me to come back." My emotions burst through the flimsy wall I put up and my face twisted with the pain of betrayal. Of heartbreak. "You made a selfish wish and it cost me my *children*."

A resounding gasp made its way around and Lottie capped her hand over her mouth. "Oh, Ben."

I stood in wait as he hung his head in shame.

"I did," he said weakly and lifted his face, his one cheek already reddening from my assault. "But I never meant for this to happen. For *any* of this to happen. I just...*missed* you."

It wouldn't be so hard if I didn't see and hear the utmost sincerity in him. How his expression begged for forgiveness, how this secret had been eating away at him and now he was forced to pay the price.

Before I could mutter a word, Henry flew by my side and lunged at Benjamin. His wide hand wrapped around my friend's throat and squeezed. A scream choked off in the back of my mouth. Ben gasped for breath, clawing at my husband's arm with wide, picnicked eyes. But Henry wouldn't relent. His vice-like grip kept its hold as he pinned Ben down on the pile of ropes.

"Henry!" I screamed. "Jesus, Christ! You'll kill him!"

Finn leaped across and grabbed Henry by the tense shoulders to yank him away. He came willingly and Finn backed off. My chest heaved as I stared at the man I married, buried deep within this grief-stricken pirate, as he sauntered toward me. His black eyes bore into me and he leaned in.

"Still think it's *not like that*?"

I fought to catch a breath and covered my mouth with a shaky hand. Ben coughed on the ground, refusing to even look at me. Henry and the people I once called family all walked away, scurrying off to go about their lives aboard the ship. Leaving me to cry in silence.

I had never felt more alone in my life.

CHAPTER FOURTEEN

I retreated to my fortress of solitude in the kitchen for the rest of the day and ate my stew there while I cleaned and prepared things for supper. Everyone else had taken their bowls and retreated elsewhere. No one was in the mood to talk. Not that anyone was particularly chatty before my confrontation with Ben.

I hated that I hurt him, but he didn't deserve my sympathy. Not now, not with this. I had no idea he felt so strongly for me, after all these years. When we'd first met aboard The Black Soul, we bonded almost immediately over a shared desire to survive. And I knew he felt for me in ways I never could reciprocate, but we'd hashed that out in England. I'd thought it was behind us.

But apparently not.

Benjamin was so consumed by how much he missed me that he made a selfish—yet innocent—wish to a malevolent creature of the sea and now we're all paying the price of it. All I could hope was that Finn was right. That we'd make landfall in the morning and find the Viking stones. Otherwise, I was stuck aboard The Queen with a crew, tormented by their demons, for the next three months.

Lunch had taken me all morning to prepare so supper would be simple; leftover stew. But I used the extra bread dough from the buns to make toutans. An old favorite among my crew, and a small attempt to bring some joy to the ship. We'd all been through enough, we should be confiding and seeking comfort in one another. Not… whatever it is that's happening here.

The kitchen door swung open and I glanced up from the butcher block to find Lottie standing as still as a statue. She crossed her arms and leaned against the wall just inside. But instead of the usual stone hard expression, I found a softness I never knew I missed until now. A side of her she rarely showed, even in times of good.

I added a fresh flour-coated dough cake to the platter ready for frying and sucked in a deep breath. "Didn't expect to find you here."

She shrugged. "Didn't expect to come." Her eyes fluttered shut as she composed herself. "But what kind of friend would I be if I let you hide in the kitchen and fall apart all on your own?"

I bit my bottom lip to keep from tearing up. "Really?"

Lottie nodded. "That was awful what ensued out there. You don't deserve what's happened to you." She pushed off from the wall and stepped closer. Her arms relaxed from their crossed stance and fell to her sides where she held them open invitingly. "I'm sorry."

A single sob bubbled in my chest and I ran to her. We collided in a hard but comfortable embrace; our arms wrapped around our shaking bodies as we allowed one another to finally open up. To release all the pent-up emotions harbored inside our hearts. Two mothers consoling one another over the loss of the children. The only difference was that I had a chance to get mine back.

I gently pulled away and faced her with condolence. "I'm sorry, too. For your loss. I'm sorry I wasn't here to help you through it."

She shook her head and backed up a step, averting her face to wipe a tear. "It's fine. I'm fine."

"Lottie -"

"Tell me about your kids," she quickly changed the subject, her voice laced with forced cheer. "The good stuff. Not all this dread surrounding us. What are they like? What are their names?"

My cheeks pinched with a warm smile as I pulled images of them to the forefront of my mind. "Arthur and Audrey. Two little angels. They're just like Henry. Strong and brave, stubborn, sweet."

"I feel awful for the way I've treated you," she

told me. "When you first arrived, I should have welcomed you back. I should have done something."

"It's okay," I replied.

"No." Her lips pursed. "It's most certainly not. You are my friend. My *family*. I should have treated you as such, especially after you told me the reason for your return."

"I thought you were mad at me for leaving."

Lottie's eyes widened. "Goodness, no. You had to go. I knew that, accepted it. I've cherished the memory of you and Henry for years." Her shoulders slumped. "I've just been so lost. Grief has completely taken over who I once was and it's just easier to not feel anything at all."

I gripped her upper arms and held her gaze. "I, above anyone, wholeheartedly understand what you're going through. Only...yours is a pain of a different nature. I wouldn't dare try to downplay that."

She wiped away more tears before they managed to escape. I could tell she was struggling to find words. The wound just too fresh to drudge up. I caught a glimpse of my bag hanging on the rack behind her and darted for it. I reached inside to pull out my journal.

Lottie's face lit up. "Is that?"

"The journal you gave me on my wedding night," I confirmed and took a seat on a wooden chair. She pulled another up next to me as I opened the pages. "I've filled it with everything important that's happened to me over the years. Every major milestone of the kids. Some are just entries of me talking to you guys."

Lottie leaned in and examined the book with wonder. Her fingertips gently ran over the pictures of Arthur and Audrey. She'd probably never seen anything like it. An actual photograph. I wasn't entirely sure, but I don't think the first camera would be invented for another hundred years or so.

"My Lord, they're the spit right out of Henry's mouth."

I chuckled. "Yeah, they got nothing from me."

She pointed at one picture of Audrey laughing. "No, she has your smile. And I bet she sounds like you when she laughs."

God, it was hard to fight off the wetness that glazed over my eyes. "Yeah, she does."

"What's this?" Lottie asked as I turned a page and a picture of the kids with Mom on the front porch mirrored a long-written entry. You could see the whole house.

"That's our home," I said. "It's in Rocky Harbour, a community that doesn't exist here yet. It's lovely and quiet. Perfect for us."

"It's beautiful." She ogled it admiringly. "And your mother? She was alright after all?"

I sighed. "Sort of. She landed on a beach somewhere after Maria threw her into the future. Someone found her, called for help. She was dead, but they brought her back to life. She took a while to heal from the stab wound and still walks with a limp, but she's good."

Lottie's face twisted in disbelief. "Brought her *back to life*? With magic?"

I laughed, a gutsy one that felt foreign to my insides. "No, with modern medicine and technology."

Lottie guffawed carelessly. "Sounds like potions and relics to me."

I couldn't really argue with that.

She rubbed her fingers over her mouth in thought. "Do they... have you told them? About anything?"

"They know they have an Aunt Lottie and Uncle Gus who lived a long time ago with Uncle Finn and Benjamin. But they know nothing of time travel or pirates. Or their *blood* relations to the past."

I flipped to a page where I did my best to sketch what they all looked like and she took it in with delight.

My throat ran dry. "I had to draw the pictures. I'm no artist, but I couldn't find anything in our history books or records. No pictures or drawings, no indication of, um, where you all ended up."

"I would almost say that's a good thing," she replied. "Aside from mine and Gus's wedding, the last few years haven't exactly been a wonder. And," she inhaled deeply through her nose, "I'm betting the next few months won't be pretty, either."

I closed the pages and handed the book to her.

She accepted it with a confused look. "Take it, read it through and you'll know exactly how the last four years of my life have been."

Lottie was quiet as she slowly pried open the pages once again and found pictures of the kids when they were first born. When they were just pudgy fat infants. I watched as her fingertip traced over the round lines of their little faces, caught how the corner of her mouth twitched with pain or happiness, I wasn't sure.

"You know," I began carefully, "What happened to you, it's common. It happens to a lot of women. In the future, we have people called therapists, and places called support groups. It helps to talk about the trauma in order to make sense of it. To eventually bring yourself to a place where you can be happy again."

Lottie shut the book and tucked it under her arm as she stood up. "I haven't spoken about it since it happened. To anyone. Not even Augustus."

I pushed to my tired feet. "Maybe that's the problem, why you can't get past this wall you've put up. Gus should be the most important person in your life right now. The one person you should be able to talk to about this. Take comfort in your husband, he's grieving, too."

Lottie tilted her head back and pointed her chin in my direction with a coy, half-smile. "You should take your own advice, Time Traveller."

My head bobbed slowly as I admitted how right she was. I was always good at giving advice but dreadful at learning from it myself.

"I'm going to put this in my cabin and then come back to help with supper, okay?" she said as she neared the door.

I just nodded, eternally grateful for her friendship. She left the kitchen and I returned to the food; starting the fire in the stove to warm the stew and fry toutans. Lottie was back in minutes and threw on an apron as she sidled up next to me and helped. We fell right back into our old routine of light laughter and meaningful banter. I missed her greatly and it felt good to have a small piece of her back.

I carried that good mood with me to the mess hall where we served our crew of friends and took our seats. Without really thinking, I reached for Henry's hand under the table next to me, but he flinched away. No one else saw the simple exchange, but I felt my cheeks reddening in embarrassment. The stark movement ripped me from the temporary cloud of joy and anchored me in the reality I'd carelessly forgotten.

The reality that my own husband couldn't stand to touch me.

***

After everyone was done eating, the crew checked the boat and then retreated back to their cabins—except Ben who tucked himself away in the crow's nest—while I cleaned up the kitchen and mess hall. It felt good to be alone with my own thoughts as I kept my hands busy.

The moon was high in the navy sky when I walked across the deck to get some fresh air before heading down to my cabin where Henry waited. I spotted Finn at the bow, leaning against the railing and peering down at the sea. After a few quick steps, I joined him. The air was different there, at the front, with the clean ocean breeze billowing around you. I inhaled long and hard as I cast my face to the sky.

"Shouldn't ye be in bed?" Finn asked and took a swig of rum from a small bottle and then handed it to me.

"I could ask you the same." I nudged his arm with mine and took a long sip. "Big day tomorrow. We get off this ship and search the land for Viking stones."

"Aye," he replied. "I ken whereabouts it is. The Vikings always had a likeness for certain areas. And with what ye told me, I reckon we will find it in no time."

"And you're sure you can make them work?"

Finn nodded surely. I believed him.

"Do you still have family there?" I asked. "In Scotland?"

He bowed his head and let out a soft grumble. "Nae. Everyone in my family is dead."

My head cocked back in shock. "I'm so sorry."

He waved his hand in the air, brushing off my sentiment. "'Twas a long time ago. Scotland hasn't been home for a long time." He patted my arm and turned. "I'm headin' to bed. G'night, *wench*."

I laughed as he ran off before I could punch him. But I knew what Finn meant. I'd resumed my old role aboard the ship. As a cook. But I was so much more than that; I was strong and a decent swordsman, albeit rusty. Still, worthy of whatever I wanted. But all I could think of was one thing I truly wanted, besides my kids, was for Henry and me to get past this divide. We were no good apart. He *had* to see that, too. Isn't that the point of the whole soul mates thing?

Then a sharp thought entered my mind.

I didn't have a soul.

The siren assured me nothing would happen aside from outliving everyone I know and love. But did Henry look at me differently now? Could he still possibly love me the same way, even though I was a soulless being? The tension between us was tearing me down, I had to confront him. I stalked across the deck and climbed below to the cabins. I calmed my breath before turning the knob and entered the room. Henry was there, waiting in bed with a single candle lit next to it. His eyes flew open and locked on mine.

"Are you so out of love with me that you won't even hold my *hand*?" I said, anger biting back all my other emotions. My chest heaved as I leaned back against the wall, eyes still glued to his.

Henry finally sat up and rubbed his hands over his sleepy face. Mauling down the back of his long blonde hair.

"No matter what's happened, or will *ever* happen, I will *always* love you as much as a human being can possibly love another. Nothing will ever change that."

My heart trembled in my chest. "I need more." He opened his mouth to speak but I beat him to it. "I know I made a mistake. But so did you. Yes, I should have told you about the siren immediately." I tipped my head. "But I begged you not to take them on the water. I told you how afraid I was. And, still, you took them on the water!" I stepped to the middle of the tiny room. "I forgave you a long time ago. But you still haven't forgiven me. We need to start there before we can move any further. Before we can move on from this anger, together. But, also because I'm falling apart, and I can't think of anyone I need more right now."

Henry's dark eyes glistened as they stared up at me from the bed. A calm sigh escaped from his bare chest. His long arms reach over, grabbed me by the waist and pulled me to him in one fell swoop. A slight gasp chirped from my throat.

I stared down as his face pressed against my warm belly and then peered up at me, his arms wrapped firmly around my hips. Slowly, I eased between his legs that dangled over the side of the bed. My fingers stretched through those soft yellow waves and a low hum purred from his chest as our bodies pressed together.

I cleared my throat and looked him in the eye. "Is

this a yes? Do you forgive me?"

Henry held my gaze as his hands reached up and slipped off my trouser suspenders, slowly trailing them down the white sleeves of my blouse. The pants dropped to my feet as he slid wide hands up my thighs and under my shirt, caressing the tender skin of my stomach.

"If forgiveness is what you need, then it's yours."

My stomach twirled with glee as I lifted one leg and slipped a knee along his hip to rest on the bed. Our bodies pressed harder against one another and fell in sync with the rapid breaths that filled the room. Slowly, my fingers fiddled with the buttons of my shirt until it fell open, revealing my anxious chest. My breasts heaved inside the bra and Henry reached around to undo the clasp in one flick. The rest of my clothes fell to the floor and I stood before my husband, naked and wanting.

With a deep growl, Henry's hands gripped me by the waist and lifted me on top of him. We rocked back on the bed, entwined together, refusing to be severed. Our soft skin melded, consumed by hot breaths and the rhythmic movements of our bodies.

"I love you," Henry's mouth whispered against mine.

I grinned with delight. "And I you."

CHAPTER FIFTEEN

Exhausted, I snuggled up to Henry's warm body and rested my head in the crook of his shoulder as we laid together, trapping the heat of our love under the blankets. The gentle sway of the ship beneath us offered a soft lull into sleep. But I couldn't possibly sleep now.

"Do you want to talk?" I asked, my finger tracing all the silver scars across his body. Some may think them ugly, but not me. They added a raw beauty to the man I loved and mesmerized me every time I looked at them.

"About what?" he asked.

"Anything. I know it's only been a short while, but the silence between us since the kids disappeared may as well have been years for how it feels." I stretched my neck and smiled up at him. "I missed you."

The skin wrinkled at the corner of his mouth and he shifted to place a kiss atop my head. "I missed you, too." His chest deflated and a low, raspy hum purred under the surface. "I never want anything to come between us like this again. You and I? We're one. One heart, one -"

The words died in his mouth.

I cleared my throat. "Quite literally only one soul, I guess." Henry didn't reply. "Do you," I swallowed loudly, "are you mad at what I did?"

I gave him a moment to think.

"No," he finally replied. "At first, yes. I was furious that you would choose me over the kids, that you would so carelessly offer such an integral part of who you are, just to save me." He shifted and my head fell to the pillow as he turned to his side to face me. His fingers gently brushed the hair away from my eyes. "But I get it. I understand now. I would have done the same, if Finn had given me another option to find Arthur and Audrey, I would have thrown my soul at those sirens to save you."

I let out a warm breath of relief. Henry pulled closer and kissed my mouth.

"I'm going to live forever, you know," I reminded him. "Never age."

Henry chortled. "Lucky me."

I laughed and shoved at his hard chest.

He rolled back and faced the low ceiling. "We'll

figure it out, Time Traveller. After we save the kids and get home, we'll find a way to make it work."

"Promise?" I asked.

"Always." He reached down to grab my hand under the blankets and brought it to his mouth. The blonde scruff tickled my skin as he kissed my fingers. "As long as I have you and the children, that's all that matters."

I sighed dreamily. "Home. God, I miss it."

Henry nodded. "I long for daily showers the most."

I deep laugh escaped from my belly and he quickly joined in.

"And fresh coffee," I added.

Henry moaned in mock agony. "You're killing me." He pulled the blanket tight up around our faces and snuggled closer. "Let's get some sleep and stop torturing ourselves with dreams of modern luxuries. We've got a lot to face in the morning and the days to come."

There was so much more I wanted to talk to him about. My soul, Benjamin, what our plan was if we didn't find the Viking stones tomorrow. But I couldn't be greedy, I wouldn't push him. Not now, so soon after forgiving me. We were in this fragile limbo as our hearts worked to repair the damage we'd done to one another.

So, I let him hold me as we drifted off into comfortable darkness.

Because who knew where we'd be resting our heads tomorrow night?

***

The black, moss-covered stones cut across the horizon as we neared our destination. The furthest tip of Newfoundland before emerging to the Labrador and Atlantic Sea. Everyone busied about, pulling ropes and packing what we needed for the journey. I'd finished my duties early and prepared the bag that now hung across my chest. All of my earthly belongings in this time.

A cold wind whipped around my face as I stood at my old post above the captain's quarters. Even though I'd handed the responsibility to Henry, I still found comfort in the spot. He leaned on the railing by my side, our arms pushed up against one another, and braided his fingers with mine.

"This is going to work," he said as his gaze locked on the approaching landmass. His hand squeezed. "It has to. I don't think I can stand three months..."

Henry's head lulled and I slipped my hand away to wrap around his shoulders. I kissed his cheek and he turned his neck to look at me with glossy eyes.

"This *will* work." I held a look of assurance and, finally, Henry nodded in agreement. We had to stay positive. Now, more than ever. "I trust Finn."

A voice sounded on the set of stairs to my right, clearing their throat to get our attention. Benjamin stood a few steps down and peered up at us apologetically. I felt Henry tense under my draped arm.

"I, uh, I was wondering if I could steal a moment with Dianna," Ben said nervously. The first words he'd spoken in my presence since our confrontation.

Henry pushed off from the railing and stood tall, his shoulders still tensed as he stared daggers at him. I placed a gentle, reassuring hand against his chest and gave a little press to demand his attention back to me.

My brow raised. "It's fine. Go, help out, I'll be down in a moment."

Henry refused to move, his hands clenched at his sides as he divided his gaze between me and Ben over my shoulder. Finally, he relaxed, and the corner of his mouth twitched as he pressed his forehead to mine. Blonde waves tickled my face. Henry's hand reach around and grabbed me by the small of my back, hugging me as tight as possible to him as he planted a deep, passionate kiss on my mouth.

After a hard second, he pulled away, stealing the last of my breath and backed up with a sly grin. The devil. I knew what he was doing; marking his territory in front of the other alpha. Or some ridiculous testosterone-fueled act. My husband's gaze flitted over my shoulder and then back to me where it narrowed pointedly.

"I'll see you in a moment," he told me, his words carrying more than just the simple message.

He didn't want me alone with Benjamin for too

long. And I didn't blame him, not after everything. But Ben was my friend, no matter what he'd done, I knew it came from a place of love. He didn't expect any of this to happen.

I watched Henry descended the other set of stairs before turning to face my awaiting friend. He climbed the last few steps, revealing that he carried a tightly stuffed backpack. It dropped to the floor and he slowly walked over to where I stood.

"All ready?" I asked him.

"Yeah," he replied. "Look, I just wanted to say I'm sorry." He peered around anxiously. "Sure, I care for you, perhaps more than I should. But I won't hide behind my feelings, nor will pretend they don't exist. I refuse to feel ashamed for loving you."

I opened my mouth to speak but he beat me to it.

"Just hear me out," Ben said. "I've been thinking about nothing but *this* for two whole days." He inhaled a deep breath. "I'm not going to Scotland with you."

A cold wave of panic rushed over me. "What?"

"I don't think I can." He guffawed. "Actually, I don't think I'm welcome. Your husband would kill me with his bare hands if given the chance. And, I might just let him. Even though it was a mistake, what I did is inexcusable, and I'll take the regret of hurting you and your family to my grave."

I stepped closer. "Ben..."

His expression wavered between regret and pure agony. "I'll help find the stones and get you guys on your way. But I'm staying here."

I shook my head. "But we need you. *I* need you. We don't know what'll be waiting for us on the other end of that portal." I found myself flung into a scattered panic inside. "Plus, this part of Newfoundland is uncharted. It would be impossible to find your way back down South."

He quivered a smile; a meager one, barely visible under his overgrown facial hair. "I'll manage."

The rational part of my brain knew we needed Ben. We needed everyone for this to work. But another part of me, somewhere in the section of my mind that often hid from the harsh reality that was my life, wanted him to stay. I'd missed him so much these last few years and I wasn't ready to let him go now. Not yet. Our time was cut too short before, I wouldn't let it happen again.

"Ben, please," I begged. "I *need* you to stay."

His shoulders rose and firmed as he held in his breath. I could see the inner workings of his mind through his gaze, battling with himself. Finally, he blew out a long breath and stared at his boots. "Then I need you to forgive me."

I'd been in his very position just a day before, begging Henry to forgive me for what happened. For carelessly handling the threat from the siren and leaving him in the dark. But I didn't mean it. At least, I didn't mean for this to happen. And neither did Benjamin.

I pursed my lips as my eyes fluttered shut.

"Fine," I told him. "I forgive you. I truly do."

"Really?" His muscled chest heaved with anticipation under the thin and dingy shirt he wore.

My expression softened and I tipped my head to the side. "Yeah. I do. You're my friend, you deserve a second chance. I would be a major hypocrite if I couldn't find it in my heart to offer forgiveness when it's so clearly needed."

I stepped even closer to him, only inches between us, and I could sense how my closeness made him uneasy. Whether of his own impulses or not. I'll never know.

"But we need to talk about where we stand," I added. "We had this discussion before, in England. But it's obvious that I severely misjudged your feelings for me. Or, at least how deep those feelings are."

Ben's shoulders shook helplessly. "What do you want me to say? I can't make myself unlove you, Dianna. I can't brush those feelings aside. And I've had four years to let my longing for your fester. It's wrong, I know -"

"It's not wrong, Ben," I quickly said. "Loving someone is never wrong. It's natural. But I just want it to be crystal clear that my feelings for you are platonic."

His brow pinched together. "Uh, on a friendship level," I clarified. "We have a bond like nothing else I've ever experienced. There's no doubt in my mind that we're meant to be friends. But," I took in a shaky breath, "*just* friends. My heart belongs to Henry. It always will. I can't possibly see past my love for him to even fathom loving another that way."

Benjamin nodded as he took in my words. "I know. I've always known that. And I'll never expect you to reciprocate my feelings. I'm eternally grateful for your friendship and all that you've done for me. I mean, you gave me a second chance at life, you saved my *soul*."

I chortled. "Well, one of us should have one, I guess."

He threw his head back with a moan. "See? You're always giving away parts of yourself to save others. You gave up your God damn soul to save the man you love. I just..." He fiddled with his fingers, picking at some dirt on his knuckle. "I just want that for myself. Someone like you."

I gave his arm a gentle pat. "You will find it. I promise."

He managed a more convincing smile this time. "So, are we good?"

"Depends. Are you staying?"

Ben turned and gawked out over the ship's deck with a grumble. "Yeah, I'm staying. I suppose it's the least I can do. I kind of owe you. For saving my life, and all."

"I think we squared away when you saved me in that alleyway in England."

Ben slowly shook his head. "Not even close, sweetness. Not even close."

I laughed and began heading for the stairs. "Well, let's start dwindling down your tab. Helping me save my kids should do it."

He followed me down the narrow wooden steps and we helped our crew finish preparations for the trip. We arrived in no time at all, anchoring just a few hundred yards off the coast of a nice-looking beach. The Queen was just too large to bring any closer, and there were no docks in sight. If the Vikings built any, they have long washed away.

I worked with a new sense of hope as the riffs between Henry and me, as well as Ben and Lottie, were mended. Tension had lessened and I could see its evidence in the way everyone worked together. The six of us loaded up our gear and lowered down into the other remaining rowboat before slowly heading for shore. When I finally climbed over the side and touched my foot to the rocky beach, I sighed a breath of relief.

I loved the sea, but I longed for the comfort of home. The stability of the ground.

We stood on the beach and stared out at the impossible vastness of untouched land, almost void of trees. Tall grass covered most of the area, with mossy mounds scattered throughout.

"Aye, lass," Finn piped up. "Ye sure of this?"

I nodded with purpose. "Yep. This is pretty much where the settlement was found. It might take some digging, but we'll find it."

Henry stepped to the front of the group and faced us as he stuck a shovel upright and leaned against it. "Let's split up in pairs and cover more ground. Finn, what exactly are we looking for?

What do these stones look like?"

"I'm nae sure." His eyes squinted as he peered around. "Perhaps, oddly shaped mounds or formations near the coastline. Their portals were for ships, so they'd be facin' the water."

"Are the stones large?" Henry asked.

"They be different for each location," he replied. "But one thing's for certain, the stones will be covered in carvings. Strange ones that dinnae make much sense to the unwise."

"Can you read them?" I asked.

"Aye, I ken a wee bit," he assured. "But I reckon I can piece it together just fine."

We split into three pairs; me with Lottie, Ben and Finn, and then Gus with Henry. Some cut through the grass to venture further down the beach and hacked away at mossy lumps in the ground with shovels. Lottie and I hugged the rocky shoreline, searching for... *anything*.

"How're you fairing?" Lottie asked me after a while.

We'd no idea of how much time had truly passed, but the sun had moved across the sky.

I kicked over another large stone in exasperation. "With the search or with life? Because I feel like I'm failing both."

"You're not failing anything, Dianna," she replied and removed a pair of leather, fingerless gloves she wore before stuffing them in the pocket of her long blue jacket. "None of us truly know what we're doing. Just trying to make it through each day."

I didn't reply, just kept turning over rocks.

"You and Henry seem to be in a good place," she added.

I nodded. "Yeah, finally. It's still delicate, but he's at least forgiven me."

"Why was he so angry with you to begin with?"

I huffed a sigh and stopped wandering to look at her. "I knew about the siren's demands for months before I told him. In fact, I didn't even tell him until after she took the kids."

"I get it," she said, surprising me. "I do. You told the creature no. You hoped it would just go away and the ones you love would never be affected. It's what I would have done, take the burden like that. It's a mother's curse, isn't it?"

I stood there in awe of my friend. "I forgot how wise you are."

Lottie grinned and bent down to turn over a heavy stone. She struggled to lift it from the ground, so I ran over to help push it. It didn't seem to be that big, but half of it was buried beneath the soil. With a few mighty pushes, we managed to pull it from the ground and roll it to the side. We both fell to the grassy earth next to it to catch our breaths. I rubbed at the tired muscles of my arms.

Suddenly, Lottie's eyes widened, and she crawled back to the cavity we just created and peered inside.

"Dianna, look at this!" She motioned with her hand for me to join her.

I scuttled on my knees and looked down into the

foot-deep hole. Another rock face was revealed, one with a partial symbol of some kind, muddled by years of dirt and gravel. I held my breath as I reached down inside and swept my hand over the cold stone, revealing more of the symbol.

"Oh, my God," I whispered and clawed at the wet dirt to uncover more.

Lottie wasted no time digging either, helping me peel back the thick layer of sod. Finally, sweat covered and gasping for breath, we both looked at each other as the cool afternoon wind whipped around our faces, tousling our hair. In unison, manic laughter cackled from our chests.

"We found it!" I cried out. My neck twisted around in search of the men. "Henry! We found it! *It's here*!"

Lottie and I hauled ourselves to our feet and waited as the rest of the crew ran for us. Shovels in hand and slick faces alight with hope. Henry reached us first, a few seconds before the rest, and stopped to catch his breath by my side. He glanced in the hole and stared at it in disbelief.

"Is it true?" he asked us both and pointed. "Is this it?"

Finn came to a clumsy halt, kicking dirt back into the hole with his big leather boots.

"Finnigan," Henry regarded him, "can you tell if this is one of the stones?"

The tall Scot knelt and swiped his massive fingers over the stone and nodded with glee. "Aye, 'tis." He glanced up at me. "Good job, lass."

"It was Lottie who really found it," I said.

"So, how many of these things do we have to find?" Benjamin huffed as he flipped the greasy brown waves back from his face.

We'd only just begun, but already we were worse for wear and in desperate need of baths.

Finn shook his head. "No idea. But 'tis a swell place to start." He took stock of the ground around us. "If this was part of a circle then the rest ain't far, I assure ye. Stones as big as this? They dinnae stray."

We only had three shovels, so the guys worked to cut sections of sod for Lottie and me to throw to the side. My back didn't take long to protest, but I stuffed down the discomfort. My hands, blackened with dirt and mud, nails stained green from the fresh grass, worked over and over to tirelessly remove as much of the earth as we could.

It took a few hits and misses, but after a few uncovered stone faces, we could visualize the giant circle that once laid here, and each thrust of a shovel was soon made with purpose. The sun hung low in the sky, casting a gorgeous purple and orange glow over the water that reflected on the land we stood upon. When the bulk of the giant circle could be seen in the ground, we all took a moment to step back and fill our lungs. The oval-shaped ring was easily fifty feet across and double that in height. Maybe more. But, as Finn had said, these were meant to have ships travel through.

"There's still one missin'," Finn said and pointed

to a spot in the rock chain that was just dirt.

"Is it just deeper?" I asked.

I walked around to the missing link to dig a little with a discarded shovel. I went another foot down but came up empty-handed. Everyone moaned in agony. We'd been searching and digging all day; we'd gone too far for this to fall apart now.

"It has to be around here somewhere," Lottie suggested. "Finn, you said these rocks were just too big and heavy to really get too far, right?"

Finn nodded. "Aye. Unless it was taken."

"No," I added thoughtfully. "No one's been here in hundreds of years. Not since the Vikings. Would they take a part of their portal with them?"

"Nae," Finn answered. "The portal wouldn't work without it." He scanned around the shadowed ground. "Yer right. It's here somewhere. Keep diggin'."

I stepped back and took it all in from a new perspective. The circle was colossal, at least thirty individual stones, surely more than enough space for a ship to sail through. But it was on the ground. There's no chance a ship would emerge that way. The nose of the boat would be pointed to the sky. I glanced up and around, examining the beach just a few yards to my back. Then it hit me.

"It's supposed to be standing," I said to my group of friends. They all turned their blank stares on me. I trudged back to the missing piece. "Look, if this is the top, then the circle would be pointed at the sea. Just like Finn said. The ships would come and go that way."

"But what about the missing piece?" Ben asked.

I thought for a moment. "If this circle was indeed once standing, then something must have hit the arch to knock it down. The missing piece should be close by." I walked to the center of the circle and jabbed a shovel in the ground. "We'll start here."

The sun had completely gone down and the moon failed to provide enough light for us to see so I hesitantly revealed my small flashlight. My friends from the past eyeballed it curiously. Cautiously. Ben couldn't keep his eyes off it at all. He shoveled the dirt as I held the flashlight dutifully. With every swing, he stared at it with longing.

"It's just a false light," I told him, but loud enough for everyone. "Wires and batteries, elements from the earth. You'll see it in about a hundred years or less."

He stopped and guffawed as his gaze went distant in thought. A twinge of sadness touched his face. "So, not in my lifetime, then."

I pressed my lips together and shook my head.

"Dianna!" Henry called from a few feet to my left. I spun around. "Bring the light here!"

I dashed across the torn earth and shined the light where Henry and Finn were digging. A squared piece of stone looked up at us and bore strange symbols.

"It's broken," Finn said and toed a small piece with his boot. "This bit here. It has part of the marking."

He pushed it against the larger piece and, sure enough, it fit.

"Will it still work?" Lottie asked.

Finn rubbed at his beard. "I've no idea."

"Well, we won't know until we actually try it, I guess." I bit back at my suddenly rapid heart. I would not lose hope. This *had* to work.

We all moved together to put the stone in place on the circle, figuring out which way it turned and fit. I held the smaller, broken piece in my hand. Everyone waited in silence. I could feel the rhythm of my heart in my ears, beating hot and quick. Thrumming against my drums. I shoved the jagged stone in place and immediately felt a force pulling it from my grip. Like a magnet. The entire rock formation lit up with a blazing icy blue light as the symbols illuminated and shook the air around us.

The ground beneath our feet began to shake and my arm instinctively shot out to grab hold of Henry. He pulled me to him, and I grasped his torso, holding us together as he yanked us away.

"What the Christ!" Finn bellowed loudly and backed up.

The earth continued to shake but, like the light, the vibrations were coming from the Viking stones. They rattled together, shaking free of the dense dirt that held them in place. We watched in awe as the circle rose from the ground and towered over us like a powerful titan. The icy glow carried from stone to stone, through the veins of the Viking symbols.

Then the illumination crackled. Like static.

A resounding gasp made its way around and we all took a step back.

"Is it broken?" Lottie asked. Gus was by her side, silent and calculating as he took everything in.

"I don't think so," I told her with sincerity. "But it's a risk." I swallowed against the tightness in my throat. I was parched. "Finn, can you read these and make sure we go to Scotland and not some random place in time or space?"

He inched closer, squinting at the many markings. "I dinnae ken what any of these are except three." He reached to point them out. "They're all Norse but, at the same time, not. This one here, it's surely Scottish. Gaelic, anyway. And this one, it almost looks Spanish." He examined the entirety of the markings with a croaky grumble. "Aye, I reckon they be places, written in Norse. Each one another portal for the Vikings to travel back and forth to their conquered lands."

"Like a map?" I asked.

"How can we know for certain?" Henry added.

Finn's shoulders slumped helplessly. "I dinnae ken, captain. It's the risk we have to take."

The ring of rocks crackled again, the light circuit of energy breaking and struggling to hold.

"We have to hurry," I said and turned to everyone. "We can take a chance on this or sail the Atlantic for the next few months. The choice is yours. I won't force anyone to come, this is mine and Henry's responsibility."

After a beat, they all moved closer to where I stood next to my husband and regarded us dutifully.

"We're with ye 'till the end, lass," Finn said and clapped his large hand on the curve of my shoulder. "Let's go save yer wee ones."

I beamed up at my friend. "Thanks. I know this must be hard for you."

"I haven't returned to Scotland since I left many years ago." He gazed thoughtfully at the glowing ring and the light made his red hair shine like copper. "I was a lad. Hardly a man, for Christ's sake. But, if I were to go back, this is a good enough reason as any."

We all stood by as Finn slowly stepped forward, one hand out, and covered the marking for Scotland with his palm. The whole circle immediately began to tremble, the blue light crackling and snapping like electricity as it morphed across the curve, pooling in that one stone. The empty area in the center where ships apparently would sail through shimmered like wet glass; blurry, dark. I squinted and leaned in, catching a glimpse of rolling hills and rocky shores. Almost like Newfoundland, but I knew it wasn't.

My face lit up. "You did it! I think it worked!"

The electric light flickered again, shooting across the loop and back to the Scottish stone. The image in the middle disappeared, just for a second. My stomach clenched.

"Henry and I will go first," I said and looked up at

him. "Right?"

He nodded. "Yes, we'll enter the portal and if it holds, the rest of you follow quickly."

Everyone loyally agreed and secured their belongings around their chest and waists as the icy glow illuminated us. Shakily, I reached out for the blurred image of Scotland and touched my fingertips to it. It felt like thick water; almost like Jell-O that's not quite set. Henry quickly joined, pushing his hand right through. A rumble vibrated in the air and we looked at one another in fear. This thing wasn't going to hold up much longer.

Our gazes locked, my other hand clenched with his, I whispered. "On three?" Henry nodded, his black eyes glistening with hope and love and so much more. "One, two, *three*!"

We both dove through the portal just as the rumbling intensified. Small bits of rock and debris fell around us. And then, for a moment, everything stopped. All sound sucked from the air and pressure from all around, pressing in on my body. On my chest; squeezing the breath from my body.

Just when the burning began, my lungs protesting and screaming for air, I was forced back out into the world and stumbled to the ground. Henry by my side. A midnight sky covered everything like a heavy blanket. The sound of waves crashing against jagged shores in the not too far distance. We gasped for breath and looked at each other in crazed disbelief as our chests heaved rapidly.

The portal stood just a few feet away and sent a

concerning wave of rumbles thundering across the sky. Broken rock crumbled to the ground and the massive stone began to shake. My eyes widened and I hopped to my feet.

But Henry grabbed my arm. "Dianna, no, it's too dangerous!"

"It's collapsing! They won't make it!"

"Yes, they will," he replied confidently. "Just give them a moment."

We stood braced together as the wind picked up, thrusting under the supernatural force that emanated from the Viking portal. The hazy middle was black on this side, telling me that perhaps it was a one-way ticket. There was no going back once you came through unless it was reactivated with the proper stone. But, after this, I doubted there'd be anything left to the ancient device.

The darkness shimmered and my heartbeat kicked up a notch as I held my breath in wait. But nothing happened. My veins ran cold with fear for my friends. Did they attempt to pass through? Were they crushed? Or are they stuck on the other side?

Or just stuck, period?

"It's taking too long, something's wrong," I said, panicked.

"Just wait," Henry assured me patiently. His eyes focused on the portal, unblinking.

Rocks continued to crumble and fall to the ground. The electric light became even more unreliable and crawled over the stones like broken lightning bolts. But, finally, the middle wavered again, faster this time, and bodies emerged from the thick, liquid state.

I counted—one, two, three, four—as they stumbled through. But one was carried; his large body slumped over in Gus and Finn's arms like a lifeless ragdoll.

Benjamin.

I bolted for them. "What happened?"

They moaned as they lowered Ben's unconscious body to the ground.

"The bloody thing began to fall apart on the other side," Finn told us in a huff. "A stone fell on his head. Knocked him out good. We had to go back for him and drag his body through."

Gus wheezed as he bent over and braced his hands on his thighs. "We almost didn't make it."

The portal screeched and moaned as it lost all integrity, and the titanic stones crumbled to the ground. The light disappeared as quickly as it came, leaving us in pure darkness. But I couldn't be concerned with it right now.

I dropped to my knees and examined Ben. His pulse was there. Weak, but there. The gash on his head, all along his hairline, however, was concerning. Even in the dark, I could see that it oozed blood profusely. I hastily dug through my bag and pulled out the flashlight. I turned it on and handed it to Henry.

"Hold this for me. The wound needs to be stitched together or he'll lose too much blood."

Without a word, Henry held the light in place, steady over Ben's face. It nearly took my breath away, seeing it fully; the blood gushing from the wound, covering his eyes and running down his neck. I worked quickly to assemble a threaded needle from my travel kit and burned the tip with a lighter. My friends from the past watched in awe, although they'd seen me do similar things before, as my trembling fingers worked to close the massive gash on Ben's head.

I made nine sloppy stitches, enough to seal the wound, but he didn't budge. He was out like a light. I wiped everything off–making a mental note to disinfect it all later–and returned the first aid items to my bag before I hauled myself to my feet.

"That's the best I can do for now," I told everyone. "But he's going to need better medical attention and time to rest. We need a place to stay."

"There doesn't seem to be anything around as far as I can see," Lottie said as she peered across the vast, never-ending hills of rolling moors.

Finn grumbled. "Aye, I ken a place we can go. It's half a day's walk from here. We'll be there by morn."

"*Morning*?" I screeched. "What about Benjamin? We'll have to carry him."

"Sorry, lass. We dinnae have a choice. There's nothing for miles."

My eyes finally began to adjust to the darkness, and the stars above shone brightly; pairing with the light of the full moon and highlighting the vast landscape that surrounded us. Scotland. The backcountry of the beautiful place. But there wasn't a hint of life to be found anywhere. My friend was hurt. We were all exhausted. And with nearly a day's journey by foot ahead of us. I felt helpless, defeated. But refused to let go of the hope I harbored inside. We made it. Against great odds, we were one step closer to finding my kids.

We just had to survive long enough to make it to the next step.

CHAPTER SIXTEEN

Benjamin's limp body jostled about as we attempted to haul him through the Scottish countryside on a sleigh we fashioned out of some thin fallen trees and a blanket from one of our packs. We only made it about a mile before carrying him in our arms became too much. He was just too much man; a solid mass nearly seven feet long. Even the makeshift gurney was no match for his size. His leather boots dragged on the ground, leaving a mark wherever we went.

The sun peeked its head over the distant mountains, finally giving us a break from the darkness we walked through all night. Finn headed the line; each step he took seemed familiar to him. And it probably was. Knowing my friend, he'd probably explored every inch of this land as a boy.

Gus let out an agonized moan as he dropped the sleigh and Ben flopped to the ground. "I can't do it any longer. My arms are about to fall off."

Lottie trudged back from near the front of the line where she walked close to Finn.

"Let Dianna and I have a turn," she said. "You guys have been hauling him all night." She looked to me and motion at the two logs on each side. "You take one, I take the other?"

"Sounds fair," I replied and bent down with her to scoop them up.

I felt the strain immediately but refused to give in. The men had done this for hours. I could do it for a short while, at least. Lottie showed no signs of distress. Clearly, I'd let my muscles soften even further beyond what I thought. The role of a happy mom, wife, baker... I loved it. But part of me longed for the lithe muscles I once sported and the strong reflexes I learned through sword fighting.

"Oh, my God!" Lottie squealed happily. "Look!"

Our heads all whipped in the direction she pointed with her chin and I caught the glimpse of a rooftop. My heart sprang to life. A house. People. We could finally stop and rest. Or could this be the hints of the property Finn was leading us to?

"Nae, it's just an old barn," Finn said. "Been abandoned for years. I've been gone a long time, but I bet it's still empty."

We trudged over a few hills until the full scope of the structure came into view. Greyed, weathered wood covered the neglected barn and the whole thing leaned too far to the right to be safe. Disappointment struck me down and my stomach soured.

"Here." Henry's hand wrapped around the log next to mine. "Let me take over."

"No," I replied. "You're exhausted. I can do it."

"Ugh, what…" Someone said with a dry moan.

Benjamin.

He stirred on the sling and blinked a few times, slowly coming back to us. The resounding sighs of relief couldn't be hidden.

I bent down at his side. "Are you alright?"

He lifted a hand to the poorly done stitches on his forehead and winced. "I feel like someone bashed my head in and my ass feels like one big bruise, but," He braced his hands on the two logs and tried to stand. "I'm alive."

"Maybe you should stay down," I suggested. "Ben, you took a bad hit from one of the stones. It fell on your head."

He glanced around, taking in our tired faces and the foreign landscape. "Did you pull me the whole way?"

"Aye," Finn said. "All night. Yer a heavy bugger, too."

That was enough. Ben didn't want to be a burden, but I knew he'd never say it. His arms rattled as he pushed himself off the gurney and I fought back the urge to slide under one of them to give support. He wouldn't want it.

"Can you walk?" I asked.

He thought for a moment and swayed back and forth on his feet. Testing himself. "Yeah, I'll be fine. Where's my bag?"

"Here," Henry replied, and Ben's face jolted with surprise as my husband let the backpack slide down over his arms and handed it over. He'd been carrying it with his own the whole time.

Benjamin accepted it with a blank look. "Uh, thanks."

He pulled a water canteen from inside and drank heavily, the water dripping down his face and soaking his beard. I turned to Finn.

"How much longer do you think?" I took in the weak expressions of our crew. We needed to rest. "I'm not sure how much further we can go."

Finn pointed to a worn path that began at the barn and led away from us, over hills and off to the horizon. "We follow this the rest of the way. Maybe another three miles. Not far."

I nodded. Three miles? I could do that. Knowing there was an end in sight, a close end, it gave me that last bit of energy I needed to do it. We journeyed down the worn, grassy path together. Every step a labored one. But no one complained. Not even Ben who brought up the back of the line.

Finally, the continuous line of tiny rooftops cut the sky and a small village came into view. A generous castle sat off to the side of the couple dozen properties. Smoke trickled up from chimneys and crooked wooden fences held in livestock.

Finn turned and face us from the front with a big smile, holding out his arms. "Welcome to Strathlynn."

Faces alight with hope and the promise of a place to rest, we followed Finn down into the shallow valley and entered the small village. Several locals gawked at us as we passed by stone cottages and I soon began to wonder where Finn was leading us. Surely there was a tavern or inn of some kind here.

But we didn't stop.

My curiosity was at its max as we came to a halt at a thick iron fence. The castle we'd seen earlier was on the other side, surrounded by trees and half a dozen smaller buildings. To enter the keep, we'd have to open a locked gate, set in an arch of cobblestones. At the top, a crest looked down on us. Three circles arranged in a bed of filigree with a long-necked bird on top. A goose? Swan? I wasn't sure.

"Finn, this is locked," Henry spoke. "Surely we can't just go in."

My giant red-headed friend kicked at the tall bushes that lined the fence until he revealed a large square rock with a flat top. He stepped on it and hopped the fence, landing on the other side with a heavy thump as his big leather boots hit the dirt. We all wavered nervously.

"Finn!" I hissed and searched around frantically. "I don't think breaking into the castle of the village we just arrived at is a smart idea."

He rolled his eyes with a thick, throaty moan.

"Just climb the bloody fence, Dianna."

I took one glance at Henry and he shrugged. I climbed the rock and gripped two of the sharp pickets as I hauled myself over. Finn held out his hands and braced me as I eased my way and joined him. The others followed and within a few minutes, we were all on the inside of the keep. Trespassers in the eyes of anyone else.

"You sure about this?" Gus muttered and secured the straps of his pack.

The sound of a gun cocking froze us all in place. My eyes widened in fear as I dared turned around. A woman and the barrel of a rifle stood by. Fiery red hair blazed against her long green trench and flowed down around her broad shoulders. The flaps of her jacket waved in the wind and teased a collection of knives sheathed around a leather belt. The gun hid part of her face, but I caught the glimpse of freckles on smooth, fair skin. She was like a Scottish Amazonian warrior, striking in every way with a mix of beauty and lethality.

She tightened her grip on the gun and inched forward. "What are ye doin'? This is private property. Ye need permission to enter my keep."

"Please," Henry said and showed he had nothing in his hands. "Our friend here's been injured and needs help, a place to rest."

I stole a glance at Ben who now leaned his failing weight against a tree.

She narrowed her big green eyes. "There's an inn back in the village."

Finn pushed to the front of our group, arms up but a devilish grin across his bearded face.

"Freya?" He lowered his hands confidently.

The woman named Freya removed the gun from her sight and lowered it the ground. I could hear the release of tight breaths all around. Who was this woman? And how did Finn know her?

She inched forward, staring at him in disbelief. Her lip trembled. "Finnigan?"

"Aye, it's good to see ye," he replied admiringly. "Yer nae a wee lass anymore."

Wordless, Freya set the rifle down on the ground and made way for Finn. He opened his arms, ready for an embrace, but she hauled back and drove the back of the gun right into his face. I gasped and jumped back while others tensed, ready for conflict.

Finn swayed on his feet for a split second before crumbling to the ground. Completely unconscious. I looked at the woman with incredulous eyes.

She slung the strap over her shoulder before turning toward the keep. "Come with me. Let's get yer friend taken care of."

We all exchanged a look of bewilderment and then peered down at Finn.

"What about Finn?" I asked.

She stopped and looked over her shoulder at the man on the ground with pure spite in her eyes. "Leave him. The bugger deserves to wake up alone. Then he'll ken how it feels."

What the hell did we stumble into here?

Nervously, the remaining five of us obeyed and followed Freya up to the keep and into the main building; a small castle fit for kings and queens. A hefty, thick wooden door hung open and I admired the clunky iron hardware against the weathered dark green paint. The only color to be found on the outside of the stone structure.

Inside, the castle was warm with the heat of a raging fire, contained inside a huge fireplace constructed of various colored stones. It anchored the main vicinity that we first entered, surrounded by common areas filled with gorgeous Victorian style furniture. Through a wide archway, I could see a dining hall lined with high-back chairs and a long wooden slab table. Servants busied about, pretending to ignore us, but I caught the discreet glares and curious glances.

Lottie leaned in and whispered. "Maybe we should leave. This feels…"

"Dangerous?" I finished for her. She nodded. "Well, Finn led us here. And he clearly knows this woman. She seems to be willing to help us."

To my left, Henry clenched my hand and I gave him an unsure smile.

Freya said nothing as she led us through the castle. We all followed hesitantly. Plaques and swords, stuffed game and tartan banners adorned the walls, hanging over doorways. Something tickled the back of my mind and I examined things more closely. The tartan, a beautiful green plaid fabric, it seemed familiar. Then it hit me.

"Freya?" I dared address. Everyone froze and gawked at me in wait. Freya turned and raised her brow, letting me know I could proceed. I swallowed nervously. "Is this where the Artair family lives?"

My crew became awash with realization as their thoughts caught up with mine.

Freya pursed her lips, but it quickly morphed into a knowing grin. "The Artair family has ruled over these lands for hundreds of years. When my father died many years ago, 'twas all left to me." She gave a slight guffaw. "Nae that there were any other choices. My brother should have been here to rule. Instead, I've been protecting the throne from neighboring lairds that come sniffing around a few times a year."

I failed to hide my shock. "Is Finn your *brother*?"

Freya rolled her eyes and I immediately saw the resemblance, brought forth by the knowledge of who she really was. "Shocking. That useless twit didn't even tell ye who he really is, did he?" She chuckled under her breath and squared her jaw as she glanced out the window where her brother still laid on the ground. "Finn, as you call him, is the rightful heir, laird to this keep and all the land of Strathlynn. He's a king."

Before we could muster a response, she spun back around and waved her hand over her shoulder. "Come with me."

In stunned silence, we followed her further into the castle, down a few winding hallways and up a set of narrow stairs. We entered a hallway lined with doors on each side and Freya stopped a passing servant girl.

"Maisie, would ye be a dear and fetch our guests some fresh clothes and towels?"

The girl gave a quick nod and scuttled off.

Freya turned her attention back to us. "Clearly Finnigan widnae have prepared ye for any of this, so I'll take the liberty. This is the guest wing, behind these doors are yer quarters. Yer welcome to stay as long as ye need but there are rules ye must abide. My keep is run by women, so get used to it. I shall be regarded as Lady of this castle, and nothin' less. Ye will not steal, ye'll be gracious, and ye *willnae* allow neighboring landowners to enter the keep." She arched her brow. "Are we clear?"

It took a moment to process, but we all replied with a yes followed by a round of nods.

"Good," Freya finished and took a few steps back to the mouth of the corridor. "I'll send a healer for yer friend."

"Oh, no," I quickly replied. She glared at me as if to say *how dare you*. "If you could provide me some clean linens and boiled water, I can treat him myself."

"Are ye a healer?" she challenged.

"No," I told her and thought of all the first aid supplies in my bag. "But I have helped fix injuries like this before. I just need some things to help properly clean and dress the wound."

She inhaled deeply through her nose as she eyed me curiously. Finally, she gave in. "Very well. I'll have Maisie send extra water for boiling. Supper is in an hour. Don't be late."

She left us standing in the narrow hallway, only lit by a few torches on the wall. Half a dozen wooden slab doors awaited us. I looked at Benjamin.

"Are you alright?"

He nodded solemnly. "I'll be fine. I've had much worse."

"Don't kid yourself," I replied. "It may not look like a major wound, but head trauma is no joke." My own head wound was still a pulsing reminder of that. "A huge rock fell on your head, Ben." He opened his mouth to speak but I beat him to it. "I'm going to get cleaned up and I'll be right over to clean up the wound, okay?"

His eyes flittered to Henry for a split second, then back to me and he gave a nod before retreating behind one of the doors. I turned to the others.

"Get some rest. Clean yourselves up. We deserve to take a breather."

"What about Finn?" Lottie said. "Shouldn't someone go check on him? You talk about head injuries being serious. Well, we just witnessed his sister drive the back of a rifle into his *face*."

I took in a shaky breath. "I don't want to anger Freya." I lowered my tone and they leaned closer. "I'll try and sneak out to see him after we get Ben fixed up."

We all agreed and retired to our rooms. Ours was fairly large with a queen-sized bed, wardrobe, and gorgeous hammered metal wash basin set in a wooden table. Copper, perhaps? An empty fireplace tucked into one of the walls. When the door shut behind me and Henry, relief nearly pushed me down through the floor. We were so close. And in a safe place. Well, sort of. I dropped my bag to the floor and slipped off my jacket as I made a b-line for the big canopy bed. The mattress took all my weight with ease as I flung my body onto it.

"Tired?" Henry kidded and put my things with his over by a gaudy wardrobe in the corner.

I rolled over and faced him with an arm draped over my forehead. "I think childbirth was easier than what we've gone through these last few days."

Henry bent down and grabbed one of my legs, pulling a dirty leather boot from my foot. The release was blissful, and I moaned with relief. He chuckled and removed the other before giving each foot a little rub.

"You're amazing," I told him as his fingers worked magic on my throbbing feet. "We're *so* close, Henry. So close to getting the kids back. If we could get Finn on his feet and find the opening to Faerie in the morning, we could very well be going to bed tomorrow night with them tucked between us."

"Hopefully that bed is our own, at home," he replied.

"Oh, *home*," I said with the tail of a moan.

I waited a beat to see what further he would say, but Henry was silent and distant as he released my feet and walked over to the window. I sat up straight and crawled to the other side of the bed.

"You know, I was worried that maybe you didn't want to go back," I admitted.

He shot me an incredulous look. "Don't be ridiculous, Dianna."

"How is that ridiculous?" I challenged. "This is your home, this time. I took you from it and it's not like you've really settled into the future. I know how much you miss this life."

He stood patiently; his expression unmoving. "And what life is that? Danger every turn of a corner? Friends constantly getting hurt because of my actions? Stealing and scavenging through a pathetic existence?"

I shrunk into a ball on the bed. "Well, when you put it that way."

Henry guffawed and glanced back out the window. "No, Dianna, I miss nothing of this time. I'm happy in the future with you. With the kids. Your mother. You've given me everything I've ever wanted."

I smiled. "Yeah?"

He sauntered toward me with a coy grin. "Yes. A family to love. A home to raise our children in." His long fingers gripped my thigh and slowly slid upwards. Goosebumps tickled my skin. Henry's face dipped to mine, his lips hovering over my waiting mouth. "A woman to take to bed each night."

I reached up to grab his face in my hands, just

wanting him as near as possible. Everything that we'd been through these last couple of weeks, the divide that wedged its way between us, it killed me. I needed Henry like I needed to breathe. The fibers of his very being have woven into mine and I'm not whole without him. Regardless of the insane, magical events that have led us here, I know I'm exactly where I'm meant to be.

With Henry.

His warm mouth took mine and my body reacted immediately; bending and arching toward him. My fingers pulling at his shirt, hauling him closer. Our lips entwined, I leaned back, and he braced himself over me. Blonde straggly hair fell around my face.

"I love you," he said quietly, but with a heavy purpose. He wanted me to know how much he meant it.

"I know," I replied. "I love you, too. I always will. Even in death."

Henry chortled and left a kiss on the tip of my nose. "That's not something you'll ever have to worry about."

He said it in jest, but I could hear the tinge of sadness laced in the words. I had no soul. I'd live forever and we still have yet to really talk about it.

"I'll find a way to get it back," I told him.

"How?"

My mind raced for any flimsy answer. "I don't know but I'm sure I can find a way. Right now, I just want to focus on finding the kids. My soul can wait."

My fingertip hooked into the waistline of his trousers and I tugged hard, forcing him to fall on the bed with me. My legs parted, letting Henry slowly nestle in my warmth, and I wrapped my arms around his neck.

"For now," I added and grazed my lips over his. A low growl rumbled up from his chest. "Just love me."

Henry's dark eyes pierced right through me with desire. "Now, *that* I can do."

***

After Henry and I spent time wrapped in one another's arms, we got cleaned up and changed with the fresh things Maisie brought to our door; a plain grey cotton dress with long sleeves and a simple shirt and trousers for Henry. He immediately covered it with his black leather jacket. His armor, his security blanket.

I cleaned Ben's head wound in the light of day and dressed it properly. We exchanged very few words and he ogled me intently as I worked. Just as we were about the leave the corridor and head down for supper, Gus and Lottie emerged from their quarters and joined us.

"Still no word from Finn?" she asked me.

I shook my head. "No. I snuck around and peered out a window down another corridor. He was still toes to the sky. I'm going to insist to Freya that I check him."

Ben snorted. "I think you missed your calling as a healer."

I searched around before leaning into the group. "In the future, this is all common knowledge. It's called first aid, and anyone can do it. Trust me, I'm no doctor. Give me a kitchen over an infirmary any day."

We eased our way through the castle in silence, taking in the enormity of where we actually were. Scotland. We'd travelled across an entire ocean in the blink of an eye and now walked the halls where Finn had grown up. A past he so cleverly kept hidden from us. His sister's words rang in my ears.

He's a king.

I kept a straight face as we turned a corner and entered the large dining hall. The table had been set for six; the five of us with Freya at the head. No spot for her brother. She had changed from the dingy emerald jacket to a lovely navy velvet dress and a long red braid dangled down the entire length of her arm. The Lady sat in her high-back chair while she eyed us, waiting for us to take seats.

"Freya?" I addressed as Maisie caught me off-guard and placed a cloth napkin on my lap. Freya looked at me expectedly. "Would you mind if I stepped out to check on Finn? He's been unconscious for over an hour and that's very concerning for his health."

She leaned back as another servant girl sliced a massive roast in front of her and dished everyone's plates.

"Absolutely not," Freya replied sternly.

Henry cleared his throat. "Milady, we respect your rules and promise to abide by them. But Finn is our friend. We're worried."

An awkward silence filled the air as we all awaited her response. She said nothing, just stared around the table with indifference on her face. Did she truly despise her own brother that much that she'd let him die out in the dirt? Finally, after a moment too long, I pushed my chair out and stood up.

"That's it," I announced. "I'm going outside."

Freya whipped a dagger from nowhere and spun it expertly around her fingers before driving it into the wooden table with enough force to jitter every dish on top of it. We all gasped and stared frozen in her direction.

"I forbid it," Freya spat. "Anyone who touches my brother shall lose a limb. Do I make myself clearer now?"

Lottie raised an impressed eyebrow my way. My crew remained seated, but I held my place standing next to the chair. The woman slowly raised from her seat and we locked in a staredown, neither of us willing to give in. When he realized Freya wasn't going to let me go, Henry stood with me.

Then Ben, Lottie, and, finally, Gus. They all came around to my side and faced down this fiery lady who stood between us and our friend. Family be damned, I was going outside to help Finn.

Whatever it took. The hairs on the back of my neck raised as I caught her hand slowly moving for the sword sheathed on her hip, her fingers gripping its hilt.

"Freya, it doesn't have to be this way," Henry tried to reason.

I slowly drew my sword in anticipation.

Again, she didn't reply, only let out a sharp whistle to carry through the keep. Within seconds, the sound of approaching footsteps could be heard and four fierce leather-clad ladies came from the next room and flanked Freya. They held a solid stance and gripped their weapons, ready to fight.

Freya smirked knowingly. "Ye think I've protected this property all these years with luck? Anyone who's trespassed on my land has *never* been given the chance to leave."

"We aren't trespassing," I warned her and narrowed my eyes. "You invited us in."

The corner of her mouth went crooked. "Who said I was talking about you?"

"Freya stop!" a deep, breathy voice bellowed from the foyer.

We all whipped our heads in the direction of him. Finn. Looking worse for wear and leaning heavily against the archway that divided the two spaces. The relief overwhelmed me, and I let the grip around the hilt of my weapon relax.

"Brother," Freya cooed mockingly, "So good of ye to join us." She motioned to her guards. "Ladies, bow down to yer laird."

The women exchanged looks of confusion but, ultimately, obeyed their Lady and gave a slight bow in Finn's direction. Freya remained standing tall.

She glared at her brother as he panted for breath. "Perhaps yer crew could excuse us while we discuss where the hell ye've been for the last fifteen years."

Finn stepped into the room. "Agh, dinnae be a bitch, Freya. These people are nae my crew, they're my family. They can hear whatever it is ye have t'say."

"*Family*?" her eyes bulged and then morphed with spiteful anger. "*I* am yer family, Finnigan. The sister ye left behind with that monster. We were born into a nightmare, one we had to live every God-damned day. But I got through it because I had ye. My brother. My protector. Then I wake one morn to find ye *gone*? Disappeared off the face of the bloody *earth*?"

Finn's eyes glazed over with tears of regret and something else, which left me to believe her words were true. He stepped closer to her and she tensed.

"Father told me ye were dead." She bit back all emotions; fists clenched at her sides.

I felt wrong standing there, witnessing their painful reunion. But Finn clearly wanted us with him. Needed us. I wouldn't leave him now, not after everything he's done for me.

"Is *that* what the bugger told ye?" Finn shook his head incredulously. "Figures. Father'd rather me dead than what I truly am."

Freya's brows pinched together. "And what's that?"

He hesitated. It hurt my heart to watch the struggle on his face. "He caught me with...a boy...from the village." He hung his head. "We were...indisposed. Father beat me right there, in the woods, until I begged for death."

He guffawed and took a deep breath. His sister stood stiffly, the weight of his words holding her in place. I knew how she must feel. I couldn't believe my own ear.

"Perhaps that was the day I died in his eyes. He sent me away after that. Banished me from the lands, from Scotland altogether. Called me every Jesus name in the book, just for being what I am. I fled to England with nothin' more than the tattered, bloody scraps of clothes on me back."

Finn pointed at us, at Henry, and Freya glanced over.

"These people took me in, accepted me *despite* the way I was born. Not carin' about who I choose to take to bed. I found a home with them; I found a family. They saved me." His boots clunked across the wooden floor and he dared reach for his sister's trembling hands. She refused to meet his gaze. "But I've regretted leavin' ye every single day, sister. For that, I'm truly sorry."

We all held our breaths in wait as Freya stared at the floor and pressed her lips together. Finally, I watched her squeeze her brother's hands tightly in the space between them and she braved to look up at him. Her hardened face softened under the pressure of the emotions she was surely battling with and those emerald eyes–the same as Finn's–glistened with tears.

Without a word, she let go of the anger and fell into her brother's embrace. He happily threw his long arms around her as she sobbed helplessly against his chest. Finn turned his neck to look toward us; catching my gaze and gave us a curt nod.

We could go now. We'd stood and supported him during this painful time, and he could take it from here. Silently, we all headed back to our rooms. Neither of us spoke a word as we made our way through the keep. How could we? What would we say? I just witnessed something incredible, something no one should ever have to face, let alone in front of their loved ones.

Finn's shocking past broke my heart and I saw him in a whole new light. I always knew he was a good man, a human being who deserved more than the dark era he was born into. But to learn of the horrific childhood he ran from, of the privilege and luxuries he gave up, just so he could be the person he wanted to be...

A man worthy of anything he wanted; a king, even.

CHAPTER SEVENTEEN

The smell of warm breakfast filled the keep as I wandered past the front windows and caught Benjamin outside, shirtless and chopping his way through a giant pile of wood. Henry and Gus were out back, helping to fix the door on an old barn while Lottie sat in the sitting room sharpening her knives. Strangely enough, she fit right in here, in this place full of women just like her. Fierce and capable.

"Enjoying the view?" Freya asked, eliciting a slight gasp from me. I hadn't even realized I'd been staring at Ben, I'd just been lost in a daze, thinking about everything going on around me.

I blinked a few times and smiled. "I was just daydreaming."

She side-eyed Ben outside and then gave me a coy grin as she held her hands neatly behind her back. "Would ye be a dear and let everyone know breakfast is ready?"

Freya turned and headed back toward the kitchen.

"Do you know where your brother is?" I called after her.

"Somewhere around here," she called back and disappeared behind swinging doors.

I woke up anxious. Today was a new day and we'd come so far to get to this point. There was only one step left. Find the door to Faerie. Finn promised he knew how to get there, and I couldn't wait another day. It had to be now.

I ventured outside and strolled over to Ben, still chopping away at a huge pile of logs. The heap he'd cut, however, was twice the size. Sweat glistened off his caramel skin and he flung those messy brown locks away from his face when he noticed me coming toward him. He drove the axe into a stump and grabbed a soiled towel to wipe his face.

"Morning, sweetness."

I couldn't hide my grin if I wanted to. "Morning to you, too. Shouldn't you be resting?" I pointed at his head.

"I'm fine," he replied. "Like I said, I've had worse."

"Are you... happy?" I asked. "I mean, happier, at least?"

I didn't know how to say it and we'd already put

this behind us—for the second time—but I worried for him. Ben loved me, a fact I'll never deny. But I always made sure to let him know where the line stands. I cared for him as if fate required me to. But my heart would always belong to Henry.

"I'm just happy you're not mad at me anymore," he replied and grabbed his yellowed shirt from a rock.

I grinned but it jarred against the anxiousness I felt over searching for my kids. "Breakfast is ready. Come and eat before we go. Tell the others."

He mock saluted me. "Yes, ma'am."

Our time together would be over soon, a thought that just dawned on me. Once again, cut short before we got the chance to really experience our friendship. At some point today, Finn would lead me and Henry to Faerie to find our kids and then we'd go home.

"Ben?"

He looked at me in wait.

"Can you..." I chewed nervously at my bottom lip and squinted from the sun. "Promise me you'll start living your second life to the fullest? After I leave? Don't let me go back and worry for the rest of my life that you're not living yours."

Immediately, he moved a step to the left; blocking the sun from my eyes. My face relaxed and I smiled at him. Suddenly, he glanced across my shoulder and his cheeks reddened. I turned to find Freya stalking toward us, a glass of some sort of juice in hand. Her beauty was so striking, with the red hair and height the same as her brother's. An emerald stare that could kill.

She grinned at us as she came to a stop. "Breakfast is gettin' cold."

"We were just coming in," I told her.

She gawked at Ben and sipped from her cup. I could tell then, by the smell that wafted over, it was wine. Not juice.

"It sure is nice to have a hard worker around," Freya said. "I only employ women, so the heavy lifting often goes at a calmer pace." She shrugged and sipped again. "But we prefer it that way. Keeps everyone safe from the pryin' fingers of the likes of men around these parts. Only wantin' two things; my castle and my bed."

I nodded and she made eyes at Ben. "I might change my mind about my bed, though."

She gave him a wink and then spun on her heel as she headed back to the main house. Ben went wide-eyed and stunned. I stifled a laugh and ran off behind Freya.

Everyone sat around the long, narrow table in the dining room and I took a seat next to Henry. His hand took mine under the table and I saw just how dirty his were.

"Been keeping myself occupied around the property all morning," he told me. "Distracted. All I can think about is -"

"The kids," I cut in. "I know. I just want to leave as soon as we can." I held his hand tightly as I looked down the table to where Finn sat to Freya's left.

"When can we go?"

"Go where?" Freya asked.

Her brother sighed and pinched the bridge of his nose. He took a moment to compose his thoughts and we waited patiently.

"Do ye remember when we were kids? Wee little things. Ye ran off into the woods one day and got lost. No one could find ye for days. When ye finally turned up, was down by the water. Ye was soaked to the bone and thought only a few hours had gone by."

Freya paled. "Yes, I remember. What's that got to do with anythin'?"

"Do ye recall havin' dreams about fairies after that, luggin' ye off in the middle of the night?"

She shook her head. "I dinnae ken what ye -"

"A couple of years after it happened ye told me ye wandered into the woods but came out through the gilded stone," Finn urged softly.

"Finnigan," Freya replied, worry in her voice. "What's this about?"

"Sister," Finn waved around the table, "We need to find the door to Faerie. That's why we're here."

She looked at each one of us around her dining room then turned a pleading expression on her brother. "No one believed me. I'd forgotten all about that."

"I believed ye," Finn swore. "I'm bettin' the life of Dianna and Henry's children on it."

I leaned forward. "A siren kidnapped my kids and took them to Faerie."

Her face flew into a panic, but she remained still.

"I believed ye then, I believe ye now," Finn added. "I've seen things. Out there, on the sea. We've all battled monsters, creatures of every kind. I believe ye came from the gilded stone, and I need ye to bring me back there."

"I don't remember where it was," she said sincerely. "I swear. It's all a blur. I just...I just remember swimmin' for hours in the middle of the night. I thought was goin' to *die*."

Finn pounded his fists on the table. "There must be *somethin'* ye remember."

She shook her head and leaned back in her chair; arms crossed. "No, I dinnae ken any more than ye do." Freya swallowed tightly. "But there's someone who might be able to help."

"Who?" he asked, and we all leaned in, listening with anticipation.

"The Keepers," Freya replied curtly.

Two staff members entered the room then, carrying trays of bacon and eggs. Toasted buns, cheeses, and tea. They set everything across the length of the table, and we all moaned at the delicious smells. All except Finn who looked at his sister with a disapproving snarl.

"*Witches*?"

Freya narrowed her eyes. "Yes. We often trade with them. We make all our own milk and cheese, as well as grow fresh produce here in the keep. The witches have herbs and spices, better game. Plus," she shrugged and began loading up her plate.

"Other things."

We all spooned food onto our own plates and began eating while Finn scolded his sister.

"What other things?"

She sighed in frustration. "Protection. From…neighboring lands owners. Lairds who want this property and the women I employ." Her brother stared at her, unblinking. "So, the witches offered to discourage them from comin' too close."

Finn settled back in his chair and blew out an exasperated breath. "Freya Aislynn Artair. Barterin' with *witches*? Father would -"

She slammed down her utensils. "That monster isn't here now, is he? I was thrown to the wolves after he died. He *knew* I didn't want this, but he left it all to me anyway. I did what I had to do to keep our home alive. Cut off all ties to trade that had any control over us. I put that power into the hands of my girls. We make, hunt, and grow everythin' we need. And *I* decide who trades for our goods. Not anyone else. I will not be held under the thumb of *any* man."

They locked in a staredown, a battle of siblings under the duress of stubbornness. We all watched, mouths full of food, at the show before us. When Finn erupted into a fit of chuckles, I sensed us all relax. Even Freya at the head of the table. Her stone-cold expression softened, and she smiled at her brother.

He dug into the buffet in front of him and piled his plate high. "I'm proud of ye. I reckon I would've had this place burned to the ground if I were laird. Ye've made it a home, a safe place. Ye may nae have wanted it, Freya, but yer leadin' like a queen."

We all settled into a comfortable rhythm of eating and drinking. And, when my belly had stretched as far as it could go, I pushed my plate away and leaned back. Finn rubbed the remnants of food and beverage from his beard and cleared his throat.

"Now, back to the witches."

"Keepers," Freya corrected. "They prefer to be called Keepers."

My mind immediately fled to thoughts of my mother. How she was raised by these women, these witches and Keepers. The thought had never dawned on me whether she was one of them or not. They've all played an integral role in her life, as well as mine. And here we were, begging to be brought to them and ask for help. Would they give it? Would we even find them? It was only by chance that Henry and I stumbled upon Martha years ago, and she made it clear that it only happened because she allowed it.

"I'll take ye to them," Freya added. "I'll need to prepare the horses, it's a bit of a journey. If we leave now, we can make it by the afternoon sun." She stood from her chair and peered down the table at Ben with a cheeky smirk. "Benjamin? Care to help me in the stables?"

He finished clearing his plate and bounded off in the direction she led.

Henry stood and kissed the top of my head. I leaned into the comfort that exuded from him.

"I'll go fetch our bags and jackets," he told me.

I stretched on my toes to place a quick kiss on his mouth and he smiled down at me as the tip of his tongue poked out to lick his lips. His chest hummed as he pressed his forehead to mine, and I closed my eyes. We were elated inside, our excitement met on the same level and I could feel it pushing us through the day. I would have my children in my arms by the end of the day. I wouldn't rest until we did, and I knew Henry was thinking the same thing.

He left and headed back to our room and I walked over to Finn who still picked at the remaining bits of food on the table. Everyone else had gone to prepare for the journey.

"I just wanted to take a moment to say thank you," I told him. "For everything you've done here. I had no idea about the past you ran from. If I did, maybe I wouldn't have let you come back."

"Agh, dinnae fret yerself, lass." He smeared the back of his forearm across his mouth. "I'm glad I did. 'Tis somethin' I've been hiding from for too long. I just feared…"

I inched closer. "That your father would still be here?"

He nodded.

"I love what you said about me. About us. How we're your family," I said. "I want you to know that I feel the same. You're like the brother I never had, Finn. And I'm so grateful for what you've done here. Henry and I will forever be in your debt."

"Aye, no debt needed," he replied. "'Tis what we do, for those we love. If me father wasn't such a tyrant, I never would've left Scotland. Never would've found the likes of you lot." He smiled wide, one that reached his eyes and wrinkled at the sides of his eyes. "My real family."

My chest warmed. I couldn't help but agree. If my own father hadn't pushed me away like he did, all those years ago, I never would have left Newfoundland. I probably would've stayed and given all Mom's stuff to the museum out of spite. Never would have found that dang ship-in-a-bottle that brought me to this very point.

With a family stretched across the threads of time.

CHAPTER EIGHTEEN

I waited outside with everyone as Freya and Ben led four horses out from behind the main house where the stables were kept. Benjamin wouldn't look at me and Freya had an obvious smugness about her. I wondered, only for a second, what happened between them out there. It was no secret she was attracted to him. But how did Ben feel toward her?

I couldn't think of it. Had no right to. I just wanted Ben to be happy. Part of me wouldn't settle if I left knowing he wasn't happy. He walked through life with his heart held out, and I wanted so much for him. So much more than the crappy hand he's been dealt thus far. He'd been given a second chance, I could only hope he used it.

"There are only four steeds," Freya announced. "So, pair up."

Lottie and Gus took a beautiful horse with a black, silky coat. I followed Henry toward a cream-colored one and attached our bags to the gear that already hung from its sides. Freya glanced between her brother and Ben.

"Unless ye want yer man bits rubbin' up against my brother for a few hours, I suggest ye ride with me." She turned, flung her saddlebag over her horse and climbed on top. "'Tis yer choice."

Benjamin's cheeks filled with red as he quietly hoisted himself over the back of Freya's steed and wrapped his arms around her. She grinned triumphantly and flicked the reigns. The horse began to trot forward and she looked at the rest of us.

"Follow me."

The seven of us on the backs of four horses galloped across the Scottish countryside that surrounded the Artair lands until the keep and village were far from sight. I let myself relax into Henry's capable arms as he controlled our horse from behind. Every few minutes, he'd lean in and caress the side of my face with his and place a kiss there.

After a couple of hours, my legs and back began to protest, but I didn't care. I allowed myself to really take in the enormity of what we were doing. Travelling across the highlands of such a stunning country, hundreds of years before the claws of the modern world took hold. The lush green rolling hills, the raw wildlife. It was a gift. One I'd never forget.

We headed toward a long mountain range and took our time climbing and winding around its jagged, barely worn paths. Freya seemed to know exactly where to go, probably from her trips to trade with the witches.

As we reached the top and began to descend the other side, I saw the thin line of the shore in the far distance. We were close to the sea, with a thick dark forest between us. Finally, we came to a halt just outside the treeline, at the base of the mountain. Everyone dismounted their horses and, as Henry's large hands held tightly around my waist as I slid down, my body screamed in relief.

Horseback riding wasn't as easy as it looked.

Wasting no time, Freya trudged over to the trees and knelt down, fanning her fingers across the mossy ground. "Sisters of the forest, I call to ye. I seek help only ye can provide."

We all stood in a line and waited with baited breaths. The temperature had dropped and the warmth that squeezed from my lungs turned to fog in the air, mixing with everyone else's. We watched the forest before us, silently. Anxiously.

My eye caught the shimmer of something between two trees, a figure appearing from thin air and emerging from the darkness that sat there. A woman adorned in natural fabrics that draped from her lithe frame. A crown of thorn and twigs atop her head.

"Freya Artair," she addressed. "Ye come here for my help and bring strangers. I strictly forbid the sharing of our location. Why do ye dishonor our agreement?"

Freya bowed her head respectfully. "Ingrid, please believe that I widnae have come if it were not of the utmost urgency." She stood tall and waved a hand in our direction. "We seek the location of the gilded stone and safe passage to Faerie to rescue two children who may be in danger of the sirens."

Ingrid sighed knowingly. "Those wretched beasts. I dinnae ken why we bother with them." Her eyes closed and her freckled face smoothed as she inhaled the frosty air around us. Suddenly, her eyes flew open and she stared right at me. "Dianna Cobham."

My blood ran hot and fast in my veins at the sound of my name on a stranger's tongue.

I stepped forward. "Yes. That's me. It's my children who are in danger."

Ingrid guffawed and slid her layered poncho up to reveal her hands and brought them together in front of her. "Yes, ye Cobham girls. Always gettin' in trouble. Always meddlin'."

I shook my head. "No, I swear. Not this time. I'm here because a siren by the name of Seneca stole my children from the future and forced me to travel back. I'm not here on my own accord. I had no choice, not if I wanted to get my kids back.

Please," I begged, my voice trembling under pressure. "I need your help. We've come a long way."

She stared at us; her expression unsure.

"What ye ask is nae easy task. The gilded stone is hidden by wards."

Henry stepped forward. "Please, we'll do anything. We can't turn away now."

Ingrid almost seemed amused. "It's protected by a sea of beasts."

"That won't be a problem," Lottie chimed in and moved the flap of her jacket aside to reveal a small armory attached to her thighs.

The witch chuckled and stepped out from the shadow of the trees. Two others suddenly emerged, one on each side of her.

"We can bring ye to the stone," Ingrid said. "But ye on yer own from there. The sea of beasts are not to be taken lightly. They're vicious, their purpose is to protect the door. If ye are somehow successful in your venture, ye need to go back to the future where ye belong."

Henry and I exchanged a worried glance. We had no idea how we were going to get home. All our efforts thus far were to get the kids. Nothing more. I figured, if we had Arthur and Audrey, everything else didn't matter. We'd find a way home, eventually.

"We would gladly do that," I told the sisters. "As soon as we figure out a way to get back."

Ingrid's face relaxed with indifference. "Just get

yer kids, Dianna. Come back to us, we'll make sure ye get home. We'll handle the horses in yer absence, they'll be waiting when ye return."

My eyes tingled with wetness. "T-thank you. Thank you *so* much."

All three witches turned their unimpressed stare at Henry and me.

"We're only doing it because 'tis our duty. And all on *one* condition," Ingrid added. "Ye and yer kin are *never* to meddle with the laws of time ever again. Get yer children and go home. Dinnae look back, ye hear?"

I swallowed nervously; I didn't want to push our luck, but I had to make sure of something. "That offer includes Henry, right? I know he's from this time, but he belongs with me. In the future."

Ingrid looked to her sisters and a range of expressions filtered across their three faces as if they were silently talking to one another simply through their thoughts.

Ingrid turned to us and nodded. "Our sister Martha made that deal; we shall honor it." She glared at Ben. "But it extends to no one else."

Confused by her last statement, I brushed by it. "Agreed."

"Very well," Ingrid replied, and her bare feet glided over the mossy floor. Her sisters followed, flanking her sides. Her arms raised in the air. "Step back, please."

We all obeyed and watched in fascination as the three witches, the Keepers of Time, hummed softly to themselves. Their toes dug into the soil and the ground beneath us began to tremble. The air vibrated around our heads and a strange pressure closed in. The mountain to our back let out a screeching moan as a crack in the stone tore apart, spreading wide to reveal a portal of some kind. As the chasm greedily sucked in a gust of air, my ears popped, and the pressure on my head subsided.

"There," the sisters said in unison. Ingrid continued. "This shall bring ye to the island of the gilded stone. From there, yer on ye own. May the universe be on yer side today, Dianna Cobham."

Overcome with spinning emotions, I bit them back and gave the women a gracious nod. Hand in hand, Henry and I led our group of friends into the awaiting portal; a dark ravine nestled in the mountain. We blindly trusted the witches but, truthfully, I would have done anything if it promised to bring me closer to Arthur and Audrey. We were about to approach the gateway to the realm of Faerie and save my children from the clutches of an insane siren. *I'd have my babies in my arms today.* A thought I carried with me as I leaned into the dark hole of energy.

One by one, we all emerged on the other side. Our feet stumbled across the steady ground as we stepped through a rift in the air. It was cooler there, full of sea mist, and the wind whipped carelessly around us. Surrounded by the ocean in every direction, we truly were on an island. Just like the sisters said. A meager amount of land made up the mass, with a jagged wall of stone in the center. Thick veins of gold trickled down its face, glowing like yellow lava and pooling in a narrow creek that led to the sea.

"That must be the gilded stone," I said and pointed the few yards away.

Freya gasped as she stared unblinking in the distance. "I remember…"

Finn wrapped an arm around his sister. "I'm sorry no one believed ye. I cannae fathom you swimmin' ashore from here." He kissed the top of her head. "I'm sorry."

She wiped her cheek and shrugged away from her brother's embrace. "I'm fine. Was a long time ago." She turned and face the rest of us. "Let's find a way in."

I glanced around. Nothing but ocean as far as the eye could see, and not a creature to be found. No magical wards, no monsters protecting the stone.

"Something's wrong," I said.

Henry stiffened by my side and a deep growl erupted from within him. He peered around skeptically. "There's no sea of beasts."

Everything was too…quiet.

Slowly, I walked toward the gilded stone and noted how the gilded veins seemed to be alive; oozing down the face of the rock like molten gold. A strange force pushed against me, a vibration in the air. I reached out and pressed a hand against the massive stone and my entire body tingled from the sensation. Magic lived here; it was saturated in it. I knew nothing of the ancient power, but some part of me recognized it. The unnatural force, the ethereal feeling that emanated from it.

"Maybe we're lucky today?" I suggested foolishly.

The water behind us began to bubble and some large, dark mass moved beneath the surface.

"Guess again," Benjamin said. "I think we're about to meet the guards of the stone."

Everyone braced their stance and gripped their weapons in wait as the bubbles grew larger, rippling out from a single source. Steam billowed up from the water and a strange shape emerged. Two glassy black eyes blinked at us from the head of a horse, one too big to be any man ridden stead. This thing must have been the size of a small whale beneath the surface of the water.

Who dares touch the gateway to Faerie?

The voice, a sharp musical one, carried heavily through the air and I knew it came from the beast, but its mouth did not move. The creature shook its head like a dog, sending water droplets flying in the wind and showcasing its slick, black, oily mane. Like tar dripping from its head.

Freya stepped forward. "We seek safe passage into Faerie to retrieve two human children. They do not belong there and are taken against their will."

As is the way of the Fae. They take as they please. What makes these children different than any others? Are they yours, Freya Artair?

She recoiled at the mention of her name, her lip

trembling. There was clearly more to her childhood run-in with the Fae than she let on.

"They're my children," I said and emerged to the front of our little group. "They don't belong in Faerie, nor this time. We're here to retrieve them and go home. Will you help us? Let us through?"

The beast's rounded eyes set on me and its nostrils flared, sending a huff of steam and bubbles over the water's surface.

We do not willingly give favor without an exchange.

"We?" I replied, confused and uneased.

The shallow sea around the horse began to ripple as half a dozen other heads rose from the water. Strange fish-like tails flapped behind them. *A sea of beasts*, the words of the witches rang in my head.

"Arg," Finn churred quietly. "Bloody kelpies."

Alarmed, I saw the creature in a whole new light. I'd read about kelpies as a child, in books of fairy tales. Mythical beings with the head of a horse and the body of a fish. Could the stuff of stories and movies truly be real? After everything I'd faced with my friends, it was hard to deny that anything could be mere stories. Ghosts and goblins, werewolves and vampires. The stuff of both dreams and nightmares. I wondered then, how much of it was based on fact.

I took a deep breath. "What do you wish to exchange?"

"Dianna!" Henry hissed and hauled me back. "Do not make deals with the Fae lightly. That's what's gotten us into this mess to begin with."

I shrugged helplessly. "What choice do we have? We need to get inside, and these kelpies are the only way in."

His mouth pinched together. I knew he didn't like this, no more than I did. I turned to the kelpie.

"I'll make the deal."

The creature rose up further from the water, revealing more of its unnatural appearance. Its tarry mane hung slick to the side of its long head. Scales like blackened metal rather than soft fur. Two horns in place of its ears.

Do you have anything of value?

"I have gems and coins," I replied.

The kelpie shook its head slowly, almost hypnotizing. *We care not for foolish mortal things.*

"I have nothing else of value," I told it.

That bracelet around your wrist says otherwise.

Shocked, my fingers immediately touched the bracelet that Audrey had made for me.

"My daughter gave me this," I said as my heart clenched in my chest. "What could you possibly want it for? It has no value."

It means something to you; therefore, it has value to us. Would you care to weave it into my mane? The kelpie asked and inched closer.

A massive black fishtail splashed in the water behind it, unnerving me further. I chewed at my lip as emotions swirled in my chest. The trinket, although worthless, meant so much to me. But it was a small price to pay to get my kids. I hardened my nerves and removed the bracelet as I stepped into the water.

"Dianna," Gus piped up. "You should take someone with you into the water."

"I'll be fine," I said, not wanting to endanger anyone I loved any further than I already have.

They all stood by, tense and wrought with anticipation. All hands were on weapons, ready to draw them at a moment's notice. I inched closer and closer to the beast, the stench of rotten fish and other nasty things poisoned the air and soured my nostrils.

That's it, the kelpie practically cooed, *just a little closer.*

My trembling hands reached for its black hair and pulled a strand between my fingers. It felt like thick slime and I gaged at the sensation. Shakily, I began to tie the bracelet to the slick strands, nearly dropping it in the process. Finally, I finished and released the kelpie's hair from my grip.

"T-there," I said, "Now will you open the door?"

The pack of beasts closed in, circling around me and my heart flew into a panic. But I couldn't move fast enough. The water held me in place as I craned my neck frantically in the direction of my friends, of Henry. My wide eyes glued to his and I saw his face redden with rage.

Just as I turned to run, a massive hoof struck my chest, kicking the breath right from my lungs. I gasped for air but only got a mouthful of water as another hoof collided with my stomach and pushed me down under the surface of the water. Muffled screams and splashing could be heard as I struggled to break free. I tried to call for help but only let more saltwater pour down my throat with every attempt.

I could feel my lungs tightening, dying under the stress of the lack of oxygen. If only I could break the surface, grab a quick breath, I could hold on for another moment. But a thick, eel-like tail wrapped tight around my torso and held me further down. I kicked and pulled, scratched at the fishy scales of the monster. But it was no use.

My arm suddenly burned, and I blinked through the muddled water to see the mouth of another kelpie clamped around my forearm. My blood tainted the water as I heaved a slow punch at the thing's face. Right between its eyes. It wouldn't budge. Again, I punched, pounding and pounding at its skull. Finally, it released my arm and swam away. More blood oozed from the wound, but I could hardly even feel the limb.

A hand came from somewhere and grabbed hold of my injured arm, hauling me away from my timely death. As my body cut through the water and emerged on land, the pain of the kelpie bite suddenly burned, and I cried out in agony.

Henry lowered me to the ground and hovered over in a frantic stance. Searching my body for the source of my pain.

"My arm!" I screeched, but I could hardly move it. The burning was too much.

Henry tore open the sleeve of my jacket in one swift rip. His chest heaved rapidly as water dripped from his head.

"There's something stuck in your skin," he said and pinched the wound. I let out another fierce scream, but he didn't let go. "It's a tooth. I have to remove it, Dianna." One of his hands grabbed the back of my head and pulled our faces together. He placed a hard, wet and breathy kiss on my lips. "Just bear the pain. It'll only be a moment, I promise."

"Just do it," I spat through clenched teeth.

Henry wasted no time. His fingers dug into my flesh and gripped the kelpie's pointed tooth. It resisted, tearing the bloodied tissue and skin of my bitten arm, but Henry didn't stop. Finally, in one last attempt, my beloved pried the sharp bone from my arm and the pain immediately subsided.

Breathless, I managed to sit up.

"Are you alright?" he asked.

"I'll be fine," I replied and stared down at what was left to my arm; the wound hung open, a massive gash where a chunk of flesh once was. An inky substance oozed from the teeth marks. Poison. "I have to get the venom out."

"How?" Henry asked frantically.

Without missing a beat, I clamped my mouth around parts of the wound and began sucking.

"Dianna!" Henry scolded.

But he calmed when I spat the poison on the ground. He watched in awe as I sucked what venom I could from my arm. One last attempt should do it. My mouth fixed around the gashes once again as I glanced over at our friends in the water, battling the school of beasts. Blood splattered in the air, mixing with the same blackened substance I sucked from my body. The unnerving sound of ripping flesh filled my ears.

"Go," I told him between breaths. "Help them!"

"I'm not leaving you!"

I spat the last of the poison on the ground and ripped the rest of the sleeve from my jacket. Hastily, I wrapped it around my arm, covering the wound tightly and cutting off as much of the blood as I could. The minor discomfort I was left with was nothing compared to the searing pain I felt only moments ago. So, I leaped to my feet and unsheathed my sword with one hand as I favored the other to my chest. I looked at my husband and he did the same. We gave each other a quick nod.

"Let's go!"

We ran back toward the water, swords swinging. Lottie clung to the back of one kelpie, daggers clawing at the flesh, as Gus hacked away at its flailing body. Freya and Finn stood back to back, swords flipping around them in unison, their fighting styles matched in every way. The monstrous fishtails of the beasts flapped in the bloodied water, one of them knocking Ben under the tow. Henry reached down and hauled him back up and the two men exchanged a look of gratitude and respect as they held a grip on one another's wrists.

The dead corpses and chunks of mythical beasts floated in the water all around us, tainting it with blood and the inky poison that seeped from each of them. Only one remained, the first that had presented itself, and it reared up out of the water in a fit of rage, right behind my husband.

"Henry!" I screamed and struggled to run through the water.

Before I could reach him, Ben leaped up, sword secured in both hands, and slashed at the monster's side. It pushed at the water as its massive body fell to the right and Ben pulled Henry away. But it wasn't dead. I watched in horror as it rose up again, weak and injured, but intent for the two men I loved.

Breathless, I ran the few paces between us and shoved the tip of my sword upward just as the kelpie came slamming down. The force threatened to knock me off my feet, but I held on and drove the blade deeper into its neck. My boots struggled to find a footing in the loose ocean floor, just half a yard below the water. Unnatural cries erupted from the creature as the remnants of its life choked from its body. I gave one last twist of my wrist and hauled my sword out of its flesh, letting the wretched beast float farther out and eventually sink to the bottom. But not before I ripped my daughter's bracelet from its oily mane.

Everyone crawled ashore, gasping for air as they tossed their weapons on the ground and collapsed next to them. Dripping wet and covered in blood. But we did it. We fought the sea of beasts and won.

So where was our door?

A blood-curdling scream etched through the air and I gasped as I looked for the source. Lottie hovered over a limp body, her trembling back to me. Frantic, I glanced around to take stock of who was left. Henry, Finn, Freya, and Ben all met my searching gaze and my heart squeezed with a sudden shock of sorrow.

Gus.

"No," I whispered to myself and ran for my friend who coddled her husband's body. Everyone else followed close behind but let only me approach her. "Lottie…"

She swatted my hand away. "No!" Her face whipped in my direction, stained with tears and blood. "Fix it! *Fix him*!"

My mouth gaped helplessly as I glanced down at Gus's blank face. His paled, empty expression. Lottie's arms cradled him, and I knew by the way his limp neck dangled, how his hollow body hung in her grasp and blood-soaked through all his clothing where his heart should be...

Gus was gone.

"Lottie, I-I'm sorry." I shook my head as hot tears stung my eyes. "There's nothing I can do."

"*No!*" she screamed again, her voice now raw as she held his face to her chest and rocked back and forth. "You fix *everyone*. Why can't you save him for me?"

My hand cupped over my mouth as I cried for my friend. For my inability to give her this. I touched her back, and she let me stay there. "Sometimes...there's nothing anyone can do. He's just too far gone."

She let out a fierce wail to the sky and fell back into my arms where she shook with every painful cry. I was right there with her, unable to hold back the emotion. I glanced behind us to find that I wasn't the only one. Henry, Finn, and Ben all stood together. Hands on their solemn faces; stares glistening with tears of mourning.

Gus had been one of Henry's first friends in this world. Loyal to the end. It killed me to watch the agony on his face as he fought back his grief. Freya was the only one removed from the heavy emotions that weighed down on us, and she spun on her heel as she sheathed her sword and stomped over to the gilded stone. Her fists pounded on the rock as she called out.

"We slayed yer beasts! What more do ye want? Open the bloody door!"

The ground trembled beneath us as a crack in the stone slowly pried apart. Right above the channel of water that joined it to the sea. The water began pouring inside as if a plug had been pulled from a drain. The body parts of dead kelpies waded together and moved toward the opening, returning to the land from which they came. The force magnified, drawing in more and more of the sea, flooding the little bit of land on which we stood. None of us had a chance to prepare for the rising tide and it soon swept us up, dragging us toward the narrow opening.

"Brace yourselves!" I called to everyone.

I firmed my grip around Lottie, and she held onto her husband with everything she had. Together, we moved toward the rest of our group, unable to fight against the current that was picking up speed with every passing second. The dark opening rushed toward me and I buried my face in Lottie's back as we were all sucked inside and thrown to the mercy of darkness.

CHAPTER NINETEEN

We travelled down the rushing river of blood and body parts, barely holding on to whatever we could grab. Rocks and debris constantly knocked into me, thrusting me off course, and ripping me from Lottie who clung to Gus like a cat. She would *not* let him go.

An unnatural light filtered down from above and I glanced up to find a sky inside the stone. In fact, as I searched the passing land that whipped by, I realized that we were no longer in the human realm. No, nothing like this could ever exist in my world, no matter the time.

Fields of blue and green stretched as far as the eye could see. Mountains made of ice, rather than being covered in it, cut the sky in the far distance.

Titans compared to the rolling hills on the opposite side of this land. Flowers as tall as trees bunched together in small forests.

Faerie. It was stunning.

I just wish I had the opportunity to appreciate it under better circumstances. Hurdling down a river of death with no idea of where we were going? Not exactly ideal. Up ahead, I noticed that the river divided into two channels.

"Henry!" I called a few feet in front of where Lottie and I bobbed down the rushing river.

He strained to look back and me and nearly went under. When I caught his stare, I pointed up ahead. When he saw the divide, he swam to Finn who was closest and grabbed on. Ben was next, and the three of them struggled to stay on the right-hand side while Freya joined them.

"Lottie," I said. "We have to swim to them, or we'll be separated."

She didn't respond, only buried her face against Gus's empty chest as water smashed against her. I took a deep breath and secured my good arm around her waist as my injured arm poorly paddled us closer to the group. We didn't reach them, but we did manage to veer far enough to stay together.

Gasps, followed by resounding moans of pain ensued as we tumbled from rushing waters directly onto a pile of thorns and branches. Brambles. They were never-ending; crunching and twisting with every move I made. Tiny thorns poked the surface of my body. But I saw a mound of grass up ahead and continued crawling. The group moved with me.

Finally, the seven of us collapsed on the comfort of plush grass. A lawn of teal and blue. I struggled to catch my breath and rolled over as I tried to sit up. I picked a few thorns from my skin and tossed them on the ground. Henry crawled toward me and I let out a deep breath as I melted in his arms with desperation. Our lives, constantly in turmoil. It wreaked havoc on the heart. But at least Henry and I always had each other. I could always find him in the wreck.

"Freya!" Finn bawled, shaking my insides before I had a chance to taste relief.

My nerves were on high alert as I searched for them. They were still in the brambles. Well, Ben was. Finn stood at the edge of the grass and pulled at his legs with all his might. That's when I realized. Benjamin was holding onto Freya. The brambles had taken her. His arms disappeared inside a pool of vines, all cutting at his skin as he held on for dear life. Ben gritted his teeth as he stifled a deep howl of pain. Sweat glistened on his forehead.

"No!" Finn desperately cried. "I'm nae losin' ye today. Nae now."

He released one of Ben's legs to haul out a blade and began hacking away at the branches. Bits of brown and green went flying in the air. I looked to Henry and Lottie, gave a nod as my chest still heaved for a proper breath. I drew my dagger and ran toward Finn. Flanked by my husband and best friend. We all chopped and pulled at the brambles as we worked to free Finn's sister.

Finally, Freya's panicked face emerged and gasped for air. Benjamin gave one swift yank and plucked her out. We all backed away as Freya went tumbling down on top of Ben. They stared at one another for a silent second until Freya burst into hysteric tears and buried her face in his chest. Ben's bloodied arms wrapped around her shivering body and we all watched in stunned silence until she calmed; her mild shaking and heavy tears dissipated into a blank expression. I couldn't help but stare at her, at her look of defeat. Life had done too much today. It was a look I knew all too well.

We all remained bolted to the ground, unable to bring ourselves to move. The quick and rapid trauma of the day's events finally catching up to us like a freight train out of control. We were constantly toying with the laws of a magical world we had no right to be playing with. Yet, we had no choice in the matter. Time and time again, these mythical beings dragged us in.

"Are you alright?" Henry asked me, his hand securing itself around the nape of my neck and holding my face to his. I could only nod. "We need to get our bearings, figure out where we are. This world is vast, but the siren can't be far. *Someone* here must know where to find her."

From the corner of my eye, Lottie caught my attention to my right; her back curved protectively over her husband's body. Gus. Our friend. He'd lost his life on this formidable journey to save my children and that was a guilt I'd carry to my grave. If that day ever came. I was immortal, after all. I should be a wreck right now; I lost my kids, lost a friend, facing death at every turn.

But I wasn't.

Did the lack of a soul take away more than I thought? Would I eventually become an emotionless monster? My mind immediately fled back to the moment I was hauled aboard The Black Soul. How the crew carried blank stares, acted without care or consequence. How Benjamin terrified me at first.

I looked at him, standing now, but still holding Freya tight. And I knew. I could still be me without a soul. Ben had found his way back to humanity aboard that ship, on that island. I didn't know it at the time, but I helped him swim to the surface again and I had Henry to keep me above water. To constantly remind me to love, to not let go of my humanity.

I stood in the still warmth that radiated from my husband, let the comfort of his nearness sooth my nerves, like an anchor keeping me in place. He didn't need to say anything, none of us did. We all gravitated toward our grieving friend and stood in a circle around her as her silent tears soaked into his bloodied chest.

I knelt down by her side and slid a comforting hand across her back. "Lottie, we...we have to go." She looked at me, those glossy blues screaming in pain. "You can stay here. With him. We'll come back for you."

She wiped at the wetness around her mouth and nose. "No, you need me."

I firmed my hand on her back. "He shouldn't be alone. I won't ask you to leave him. We'll be fine. The worst of it has to be over, I'm sure we can find the siren from here."

She pursed her lips as more tears filled the line. "Are you sure?"

"Stay here, protect his body. We'll come back for you and we can bring him back together. Give him a proper burial."

At those last words, Lottie shook in my arms and let go of it all. Whatever was holding her back. And I let her expel those emotions in my embrace, I wouldn't let go until she pulled away. It was all I could do in the moment, for my own blood waited to be saved. Somewhere in this foreign land.

"Do you have a weapon?" I asked her and she tipped her head with an eye roll. At least she was still in her right mind.

"I'll be fine," she replied. "Go save those babies."

I smiled at her and slowly stood to my feet before turning to the rest of our group.

"Where do we start?" Finn asked.

I craned my neck and really took in the enormity of where we were. Faerie. The land of magical creatures. The stuff of old tales. In a swift glance, each of the four seasons could be seen, holding the land. Icy mountains with snowy valleys. A tropical rain forest in the distance. Summer. A massive, jagged black castle anchored a plain of wasteland but was nothing compared to the sheer size of a grand structure on the farthest end of where our view could stretch. I didn't want to meet the things that occupied either of the buildings.

From the grassy mound we stood on, the viewpoint was perfect. I could see all around us and in the center of this unbelievable land sat a large body of water. The other channel of the river must have led there. We could make it if we walked around the long way.

I pointed. "There. If you were a creature of the sea, where would you hide?"

Henry brightened. "A lake."

"Let's go then," Benjamin insisted, Freya close to his side.

Together, we trudged through the fields of sapphire, keeping the lake in our sights. With every step, my heart beat faster and faster, eager to get to the water. Arthur and Audrey had to be there. I wasn't sure I could handle facing another wall of disappointment. I was holding on by a thread as it was, and it wouldn't take much to break it.

As we stepped onto the pure white sand of the beach that surrounded the lake, I held my breath as I searched around in anticipation. But there wasn't a creature in sight. No siren. No children. Not even so much as a bird to be found. An eerie absence of sound held us in place.

"Something feels off," Henry said quietly.

We all stood still, tensed and alert.

Benjamin grumbled. "Then I bet we're right where we should be."

A small bubble blipped on the water's surface and a series of ripples cascaded out from it. Soon, a rounded shape emerged with two iridescent eyes blinking wickedly at us. The siren. She ignored everyone and stared pointedly at me as her face rose from beneath the water and grinned slyly.

"Dianna Cobham," the creature cooed, her voice dripping deviously. "What took you so long?"

"Where are my kids?" I stepped forward but Henry gripped my arm.

She completely ignored my question and turned to Ben. "I take it things aren't going as planned?"

He shook his head in confusion. "I didn't plan any of this, Seneca."

She hissed at the mention of her name. "Are you not happy with your wish?"

"I never wished for this!" he yelled. "I was mourning, and you took advantage of that. You tricked me and now everyone I care for is paying the price of your actions." He clenched his fists and stared at the beast in the water. "Why? Why did you do this?"

Seneca's body fully emerged and her see-through form stepped onto the sand on which we all stood. "It is my nature, Benjamin Cook. To toy with the lives of mortal beings. You were so easy to play with, too. You and your broken heart. You didn't even notice how I called to you each night."

Henry let go of my arm and stepped toward her. "Give us our children! If you've hurt a hair -"

Seneca flung her arm out straight toward Henry, sending a wave rippling through the air. The invisible force knocked him back and I leaped for him just as he smashed to the ground.

"Do not come here, to *my* home, and demand things of me," she bellowed. "I could crush you all with a flick of my wrist." She narrowed her gaze around our circle. "Let that be a warning to you all."

"Please," I begged. "Just tell me they're okay. Tell me they're... alive."

"Your children have been right here this whole time, Dianna," the siren assured me angrily. "No harm has come to them. They are of no use to me dead."

She waved her hand in the air and peered over my shoulder. I twisted in the direction she stared and saw more brambles, green ones with neon pink flowers sprouting along the vines. They moved like slow snakes, as if alive–part of me wondered if they really were–until a large wooden box was revealed. It rose up from inside the thicket and two little bodies were curled up inside.

My heart sprang to life.

But the second I made a move for them, the vines swallowed them up again and the box disappeared.

"*No!* Give me my children! *Please!*" I shrieked and fumbled backward where Henry caught me. It was too much.

"You think I did all of this just so I could hand them back?" Seneca asked rhetorically. "You can have your precious offspring. But I require something in return."

A deep growl vibrated in Henry's chest. "No deal, beast. This is your doing. We owe you nothing."

"Is that so?" Seneca's head snapped toward him and her big, watery eyes filled with darkness. Rage. Something I quickly learned about the sea creatures. They weren't void of emotion. Instead, it swam around in their fluid bodies like colors of ink. "A debt has been owed to me for decades and no one has thought to repay it. I'm tired of waiting. I want the debt paid."

"What are you talking about?" I asked her. Every inch of my being strained against the will to run for my kids and rip away at the prison of vines. "What could you possibly want?"

Seneca lowered her brow as she peered at me, her teeth gritting together as a crooked finger formed and stretched toward me.

"You," she replied curtly. "Your mother stole one of my pearls many years ago, without making a deal." She tipped her head at Ben. "And we all know what happens when you steal from a siren."

He swallowed nervously and avoided looking my way.

I shook my head in confusion. It still didn't add up. "So, what do you want with me, then? Why coerce me to come back? Why not my mother?"

"You of all people should know, Dianna. The way

to break a mother's heart is through her children." Seneca sighed, an intentional reflex, I'm sure. I highly doubted these beings actually need to breathe. She waved her arm at her side, indicating to the lake. "You see this? It's the heart of Faerie. Through it, you can travel anywhere in the world. In this realm and the human one you all come from." Her eyes darkened even more. "Unless you're cursed and bound to it. Like I was for too long. The young Seelie Queen set me free a few years ago and I've spent my freedom roaming the seas."

She sauntered toward us and we all stepped back.

"But I grew weary of that. Of the loneliness. Being an outcast among my own. My sisters refusing to accept me back. I'm simply tired of this life, of this fluid body. I wish to walk on land, as you do, Dianna. I want *your* body."

"You can't," Henry spat.

"Oh, I can," the siren replied confidently. "And I will. Now that her body doesn't possess a soul, I can take it and still live forever, in the form I long for."

"That's it!" Ben shouted and pushed to the front of our group, so he was face to face with the beast. "Seneca Saye." Her full name on his lips sent her wailing to the sky. "I demand you release those children and let us all go."

Tendrils of water flew out around her form, like bolts of lightning as her rage ensued. Two black almond-shaped eyes cut into Benjamin and she succumbed to the cries that forced from her body. As if she fought with her own self. Two resolves in one being; one completely mad, one somewhat sane. Perhaps years of imprisonment turned her crazy. I wondered then, what could she have possibly done to be given such a punishment.

"Seneca Saye!" Ben yelled at her again. "I command you!"

A rush of broken wails and hissing seeped from every inch of the beast and her hands shook as they fought to listen to the demand. A magical bind only Ben could inflict because she'd willingly given him her name. Big mistake, lady.

The mess of vines moved again, retreating and revealing the wooden box that held my children inside. My feet couldn't move fast enough as I ran for them, but Henry pushed me to the ground before I could reach them. Sand kicked up around me and I looked over to witness the sea creature collide with my husband; every drop of her sinking into his body. Henry's arms shot out at his sides and his chest reached for the sky as he struggled to fight the mythical being that suddenly resided inside of him.

"Henry!" I screamed and struggled ot my feet. Finn held me back.

"Don't, lass," he said. "Let him fight it. Unlike ye, Henry has a soul. She cannae stay in there for long."

"S-she was going to take my body, wasn't she?" I

said, the words drying up in my throat as I stared incredulously at my husband while he took on the fate intended for me.

He trembled as he fought against her, the sea siren that didn't expect to jump into an occupied body. His face reddened from the pressure, eyes bulging. Hands clawing at the air. Finally, he fell to his knees in the sand and braced himself on his hands. His back arched violently as he heaved empty breaths. After a series of painful gags, Henry's jaw forced open even further and a milky substance spewed from him, pooling on the ground. We all stared in breathless shock.

Was she dead?

"T-the… kids, *Dianna*," he struggled to say, barely loud enough for me to hear.

But I did. I didn't want to leave him, not like this. But our two children lay in a box a mere few feet away. If I didn't go get them, Henry would never forgive me. I've made nothing but one stupid decision after another lately. But not this time.

"Stay with him," I told Finn and he nodded dutifully.

I ran to the edge of the woods where the cavalcade of twisted vines lay open around the wooden cradle and I fell to its side. With shaking hands, I reached inside and wrapped an arm around each of them. Arthur and Audrey. Two extensions of my very being. Touching them clicked something in place inside of me. A finality. A wholeness. They were real, they were here. In my arms.

Still sleeping, I scooped them both into my lap and held them tightly as I kissed the tops of their little blonde heads. Finn and Ben walked toward me, each with an arm holding Henry up. They gently lowered him to my side, his eyes filled with tears as he looked to them and then to me.

"Are they…"

I closed my eyes and felt their tiny hearts beating in my palms. "They're alive."

He succumbed to the heavy sobs that erupted from inside and wrapped his arms around the three of us. We cried together; tears of relief and joy. But also, ones to release the constant stream of fear that possessed our veins for days. The weight of it all crashed down around us as our three friends stood by, keeping a distance and allowing us to have this moment.

Audrey stirred in my hands and slowly tipped her head upward as he rubbed tired eyes.

"Mommy?" she questioned weakly.

Henry and I both lit up.

"Yes, baby," I told her. "Mommy and Daddy are right here."

"Where did you go?" she replied groggily.

"It doesn't matter," I said and wiped the hair from her face. "I'm not going anywhere ever again."

Our losses, our wins. This life we came from and everything we've ever faced in the name of who and what we love. None of it mattered in that moment. I would have done it all again to save these two creatures in my arms and the man who held us as if we were the whole world.

But, as I profusely kissed my children and basked in this moment of joy with Henry, I remembered where we were and the people who stood by, waiting to go home. They'd risked everything to help me. It was time to face everything else that awaited us on the other side.

It was time for us all to go home.

CHAPTER TWENTY

The morning sun crept in through the window of our room and warmed my face as I laid there and stared at my sleeping family. Henry, his usual brooding expression now slack as dreams filled his head. The two kids nestled between us. Neither of them stirred all night. Unlike me, who laid there, wide-eyed for hours. We had the kids back but fear still possessed me. I was afraid some new magical being or force would rise and rip away everything I loved.

We worked so hard to get here, to have it all back. Clawed our way into Faerie, and then back out again. After a quick deliberation, we determined that the safest way out was back the way we came. The siren mentioned something about the lake being a portal to anywhere in the world but that was a power we knew nothing about, and I simply couldn't risk coming out on the other side of the planet, in who knew what time.

With a kid in each of our arms, Henry and I led the group back to where we left Lottie. Ben and Finn helped carry Gus's body while we trudged along the river's edge toward the opening in the stone. Thankfully, it was still ajar, and a random boat waited for us on the beach. *The witches*. They said they'd take care of everything in our absence and I said a silent thank you to them.

Everything was a blur after that. We made landfall by dark and rode the horses back to the Artair keep. No one spoke a word as we all headed to the privacy of our rooms where we could fall apart in peace. Lottie's loss was great, and my heart ached for my friend. But she insisted on being alone.

Freya immediately ordered one of her servants to fetch the undertaker from the village in the morning to help prepare Gus's body for the funeral. She was the last to retire for the night and I wondered just how much our wretched adventure affected her. She still had that same blank expression as when Ben pulled her from the brambles. The reality of what truly happened—almost losing her life—obviously had yet to catch up with her.

I wondered about that, about it all, as I laid there

and let my breathing fall in line with Henry's in an attempt to calm myself. In a few hours, we'd be putting Gus's body to rest then heading out in search of the witches who promised to help us get home. Today would be another full of goodbyes and I wanted to relish in this moment of peace for as long as I could.

A gentle knock came at the door, stirring Henry from his slumber. His tired eyes pried open and immediately searched for the kids. When he realized they were still there, he looked to me with a questioning look.

"Probably just Maisie letting us know breakfast is ready," I said quietly and crawled out of the warm bed.

I opened the door, but it was Freya who stood waiting. Her shell-shocked expression now gone, replaced with one of pity.

"Mornin'," she greeted sadly. "Apologies. We wanted to let ye two rest with the children for as long as we could."

My brow pinched together. "Is everything alright?"

"They're here," she replied.

I shook my head. "Who?"

"The Keepers," she told me, and my heart raced. "They're here for ye."

"Already?"

No, I still had so much I wanted to do, to say before we went back to the future. So many goodbyes, proper ones this time. And Gus's funeral. I wanted to be there for Lottie, and I knew Henry wouldn't want to go without paying his respects to his oldest friend.

"I'm sorry, Dianna," Freya said sincerely and wrought her fingers together in front of her beautiful blue cotton dress. "I wish I had more time to get t'know ye. I regret wastin' the time we did have with spite and anger." She went to leave, but something held her in place. Unfinished words. "I want to thank ye. For bringing Finn back to me. I thought my brother died years ago and that feeling, that *loneliness*, it was eatin' me up inside. He never would've come back if it were nae for ye."

I nodded, hiding everything I felt inside. "It's okay, Freya. I wish..." I chastised myself for using the word. "I'd hoped we would have more time, too. I'm glad Finn came home, even though the circumstances aren't exactly ideal."

She managed a weak smile and I matched it.

"Tell them we'll be down shortly," I said with as much cheer as I could muster. Which was hardly any at all.

Freya gave a nod and disappeared down the corridor. I closed the door quietly.

"We have to go, don't we?" Henry whispered from the edge of the bed. The kids were still sound asleep.

"Yes," I replied and hugged my chest. "Apparently they're downstairs waiting. The witches."

He stood and grabbed his trousers from the floor

before hauling them on. In one swift move, Henry was in front of me, a hand slipped around the back of my neck, and kissed me tenderly. His lips lingered on mine and I closed my eyes, letting his touch soothe my racing heart. His rock-solid calmness, the gentle frequency that often radiated from him always settled me and I took comfort in it.

"Go down and speak with them," he whispered. "I'll stay with the kids and pack our things."

I pressed my mouth to his once more. "I love you."

His dark eyes sparkled. "And I you, Time Traveller."

I got dressed and ran downstairs, past the dining room full of the food my friends ate, to find three women standing in the foyer, waiting. I couldn't tell if they were impatient or if the stern look of disapproval was just their expression of choice. Regardless, they got right to business the second I approached them.

"Dianna Cobham," the one in the middle spoke. The one from the woods. "It's time. Ye have what ye came for. Say yer goodbyes and come with us. Ye must go back to where ye belong."

"Can't we have just one more day? Or just a few hours?" I pleaded. "We lost a friend yesterday. I want to say a proper goodbye, at his funeral."

"We're very sorry for yer loss," the witch replied. "But we cannae allow ye to stay any longer. The sanctity of time must be upheld."

Finn entered the foyer, his beard wet around his mouth with remnants of breakfast. "What's this? Yer leavin' so soon?"

"We have to," I told him, fighting back the wave of hot emotions that came over me. I had it all planned out in my head. The goodbyes. I'd do them right this time. No rushing. But time waits for no one, I guess. "Thank you, for everything. I-I love you so much, Finn. I meant what I said, you're like a brother to me. I owe you my life ten times over."

He grabbed my arms and tossed me into his massive embrace, crushing me against his chest. "Aye, Traveller, dinnae worry about any of that. Just promise me ye'll stay outta trouble."

Henry came down the stairs then with the sleepy kids in tow. They peered around in confusion and awe, completely unaware of the world around them. I'd explain it all to them one day; when they were old enough to understand. Ben and Lottie stood from the table in the large open space that connected to the foyer and came toward me with Henry and the kids. The witches waited patiently.

I stepped aside with Lottie. "I'm sorry we can't stay for the funeral." My stomach twisted in a hard knot. How could I say goodbye to her? To this miraculous woman who lost everything. I was about to leave her in the past to wallow alone. "I wish... I hoped to stay a little longer. To be there for you, through all of this."

The skin around her eyes was red and puffy. I knew then she'd been crying all night. But she managed a meek smile for me and took my hand. "You've got far bigger things to take care of than a full-grown woman, Dianna." Her fingers squeezed around mine and she stole a peek at my children. "Those two babies are everything. Take them home and love them every single day of your life. Okay? For me?"

I nodded. Emotions bubbled in my chest, clawing to the surface.

"Daddy," Arthur said and tugged at Henry's sleeve. "Who are these people?"

Henry set down our bags and kneeled between our two kids, pointing at Lottie first. "Well, it's a long story, one your mom and I will tell you one day, but this right here is your Auntie Lottie."

"The one from Mommy's book?" Audrey piped up and glanced at Lottie with a big grin. "You're even prettier in real life."

Lottie let out some unexpected laughter. "That reminds me," she said and reached into the large pocket of her skirt. She pulled out my brown leather journal and handed it to me.

"No," I said, shaking my head. I put my hand on it and pushed it back toward her. "Keep it. Read the stories, look at the pictures and know that you're missed."

Henry cleared his throat, saving me from erupting into a fit of tears I know I could never stop once they began. "And this gentleman right here," he said to the kids and stood to clap Finn on the arm, "Is your uncle Finnigan. Do you remember his picture from the book?"

Finn waved with an enormous goofy grin on his face.

They stared at the giant red-headed Scotsman with wonder but nodded. Audrey peered around the room until she spotted Ben hiding in the back, leaning against the wall by himself.

"And that one is Benjamin Cook, right?" she said, then appeared confused. "But where is the other one? Uncle Gus."

Lottie swooped in and squat to their height. How she managed to smile in a time like this was beyond me. Her strength was one I could never match. "Uncle Gus isn't here. He...had to go away. But he would love to be here right now, to see you both. I just know it."

"Will you tell him we came to visit?" Audrey asked innocently.

Lottie's eyes filled with tears, but she kept a happy face for them. "I promise. I'll...tell him later today."

That was it, the breaking point. Lottie swiftly stood and spun away from my children to spare them the sight of her tears. It would only stir more questions, ones we couldn't really answer. They were asleep in our arms the whole way back yesterday, only waking for short periods of time. Too disoriented to notice the body we shielded from them.

Henry and I exchanged a quick glance and I inhaled a long, deep breath before peering down at those two angelic faces.

"Can we go home now, Mommy?" Arthur asked. "I miss Grandma."

"Yes," I told him. "I just have one more person to say goodbye to."

Freya stepped in then, seemingly happy to help in the sea of sadness. "You two must be famished. How about ye run over there and grab whatever ye like from the table?"

Both bolted for the dining room with squeals of delight and rummaged through the plates of baked goods and scrambled eggs like a pair of hungry puppies.

"Thank you," I told Freya.

"Aye," she replied. "They may be children, but they're no fools. They can sense the grief in the room. Food is always a sure way to distract wee ones." She motioned to Ben in the back. "Ye got one more left, dinnae leave him with so little this time."

My pulse raced in my ears. How much had Ben already told her?

Henry slipped an arm around my back and kissed my forehead. "Go, have your goodbye with him. Leave on good terms, the man has more than made amends for his foolish wish. I'll take the kids outside."

It may not have looked like much to most people, but to me...Henry's words were everything. They offered trust and acceptance. Of both myself and the feelings Ben made no secret of. There were so many different kinds of love in this world, and it wasn't Ben's fault that his and mine didn't match. Still, I cared for him, nonetheless. And Henry loved me enough to trust me. Respected me enough to give me this moment with my friend, to say goodbye without a watchful eye overhead.

"I love you," I told him.

As the witches exited without a word, Henry gave a slow, understanding nod and turned to scoop up our bags. He called to the kids and they chased him outside, arms full of buns and cheeses. Lottie had already disappeared, and Finn followed close behind my husband, Freya in tow.

Ben and I were alone.

I walked across the room, my nerves all over the place. He toed at a loose piece of stone on the floor and peered up at me from beneath his thick, dark brow. Those lovely chestnut waves covering parts of his face.

"So, I guess this is goodbye, sweetness."

"Yeah," I replied and stopped just a foot from him. "I, uh, I wanted to make sure you're going to be alright. After I'm gone."

He sighed and flipped the hair away from his face. "Oh, I'll be fine, I reckon."

I could hear the sarcasm laced in every word. "Ben, I just...I want you to know that I really do forgive you." I guffawed. "I'm not sure I ever was mad at you."

"You should be." He pursed his lips.

"I know," I said. "Any sane person would be

furious for what you've put us all through. But I can't bring myself to do it. To be angry with you."

I inched closer and his breath hitched.

"Do you remember what you said to me?" he asked. "When you were climbing over the side of The Black Soul that final day?"

I swallowed nervously. "I said we'll always be friends."

His hair scratched against the loose linen shirt he wore as his head shook. "No, not that. The part where you said...in another time, another life -"

"That maybe we would be more." I nodded and pressed my lips together as I tore my gaze away.

"Did you mean that?"

"Yeah, I did," I assured him. "And I still mean it, Ben. I truly do. There's something about us, about our very souls. We're connected in some way, I'm sure of it. I just don't understand it."

He chortled and looked at me sheepishly. "What about now? Your soul..."

My stomach sank. "I may not have it, but it's still out there somewhere. It still recognizes yours. We saved each other from the wrath of magic and the horrible mistakes of our family. That's something that will always bond us in a way I simply can't share with anyone else."

I placed my hand over his and he stared at it intently.

"Now, I'm going back to where I belong with the man I love and the children who are my whole world," I told him. "With or without a soul, I'm going to go home and live my life to the fullest. I hope you do the same. *Live*, Ben. Find love, make mistakes, learn, *do* something with this second chance you've been given."

"I will," he promised. "I just wish -"

I cupped my hand over his mouth with wide eyes and laughed. "Stop saying that word!"

He chuckled against my palm and I slipped it away.

Benjamin's whole chest heaved with a massive sigh of acceptance. He gently pushed at my chest. "Come on, let's ask those scary witches to send you back to the future."

He slung an arm over my shoulders and led me outside to where everyone waited. Even Lottie, who managed to conceal her grief again, enough to see us off. The three witches, the Keepers of Time, stood in a triangle off to the side; a shared look of impartialness on their faces. I broke free of Ben's hold and joined Henry and the kids.

The leader of the trio of women stepped forward and slipped her hands out of her long, emerald sleeves. "Are ye ready?"

"Yes," I told her with certainty. "Let's get this over with."

She held out her arms and waved two hands in the air as her sisters followed in the same fashion. The void began to shimmer, like wet glass, until a tear appeared and ripped a hole to another world. Another time. A woman, my mother, leaned against a rock on the beach behind our home. The sea breeze whipping her black curls around her face.

"Grandma!" the kids squealed together and ran for the opening in the air. Henry grabbed hold of their shirts and held them back.

"Wait for Mom and Dad," he told them.

"Let them go," I said. "They're excited."

"It's perfectly safe," the witch assured.

Arthur and Audrey both ran through the portal, right into Mom's arms. She fell to her knees with relief and hugged them tightly as she peered through the opening on her side. I wondered if she could see us.

"But 'tis a temporary, one-way portal." The witch narrowed her eyes directly at me. "There's no comin' back this time, Dianna. Make peace with that."

"I know," I said with finality. This was it. The last goodbye. The last time I'd see any of the people I've come to call family. I turned to them. "I was no one before I met you guys. It some ways, my life never truly began until I was hauled aboard The Devil's Heart. Take care of one another, okay?"

Henry stood tall and regarded our friends proudly. "It was an honor to sail with you, Finnigan. I'm glad you finally made it home. Charlotte, stay strong. Let your heart heal properly, don't hold in the anger of loss. Gus was a good man; he wouldn't want to see you suffer."

She brightened under the mask of grief she failed to hide.

Henry held out his hand for Freya to shake. "Freya, thank you for all you've done. For your hospitality. I regret not having the time to truly get to know you."

"'Twas my pleasure," she replied and shook his hand before leaning against her brother's arm. "Thank ye for bringing my brother home."

Henry then sighed and walked over to Ben. "Although we may not always see eye to eye, I'd like to leave knowing we were friends in the end. You...saved my life out there with the kelpies." He held out an arm, a peace offering. Without a word, Ben grabbed hold of it and the two locked in a manly grip.

"Take care of her," he told my husband.

Henry's mouth twisted into a knowing grin. "Until my last breath."

They let go and Henry walked back to where I waited by the portal entrance. We took each other's hand and he stepped through first, pulling me along. But the moment my fingertips touched the wavy force field, I lost Henry's grip as his hand slipped from mine. His head whipped back in panic, eyes wide as he stood on the other side and stared back at me. I touched the portal, but it was like a solid piece of glass. I wasn't able to pass through.

"What's happening?" I shrieked and smacked my palms against the opening. Henry viciously beat on it from the other side to no avail. I looked to the witches in horror. "Why can't I get through?"

They all looked as equally stunned as I felt, less

the panic.

"What did you do?" I yelled at them.

The leader's shoulders tensed. "I'm nae sure, Dianna. Yer husband and children passed through without trouble." She pinched her lips in thought, her eyes drifting away with a calculated haze. "Only..."

"*What*?' I cried.

She regarded me curiously, almost...examining me. Suddenly, the witch's green eyes lit up with disbelief. "How?" She neared me and tipped her head with a look of pity. "Oh, Dianna. What have ye done?"

I shook with fear. "What's the matter? What's wrong?"

She exchanged a glum look with her sisters. "Only those with a soul can travel the threads of time."

I backed away slowly, head shaking back and forth in denial. "No..."

From the other side, I could hear Henry's muffled cries. I pressed my hands against the portal again, hoping he could hear me.

"I can't," I said loudly. His expression morphed in the same twisted disbelief mine surely showed and I knew he could hear my words. "Not without my soul."

His dark eyes flew open and he stared angrily over my shoulder at the witches. "Help her!"

"We do nae deal with life and death," the witch said. "Only the sanctity of time and nature. We're...sorry. There is nothin' we can do unless

Dianna gets her soul back."

The portal shimmered and began to slowly close in on us. I pounded on the glass-like opening.

"I love you!" I screamed. "I'll find a way! I promise!"

"Dianna!" Henry bawled as he violently beat his fists against the magical hole while it continued to close in on us.

Behind him, I could hear the cries of my children calling for me and my heart ripped in two within my heaving chest. I pressed my hand against the portal until the very last shred could be seen until it narrowed down to nothing and disappeared, leaving me stranded in the past while my family was safe in the future. At least I had that. The assurance of knowing they were safe.

Still...I fell to the ground in a heap of sobs as cries wretched from my body.

Lottie dropped to my side and wrapped herself around me in an attempt to conceal the vehement shaking that took control of me. When would it all end? The turmoil. The heartache. I was only human, and my mortal heart could only take so much.

"We're truly sorry, Dianna," the witch spoke.

It was the first time I'd witnessed her show a fault in her solid demeanor. They really had no idea this would happen. The all-seeing beings entrusted with the sacred responsibility to protect time didn't see this coming. I couldn't look at them, at anyone. I buried my face in my hands.

"We cannae help ye travel home without a soul," the woman reminded me. "But we still reserve the responsibility to get ye there." I tore my hands away from my face and looked up at her. "If ye can somehow get ye soul back, call to us and we shall send ye home. This I swear."

I shook my head incredulously. "But...how do I do that? I traded my soul to save my husband."

Benjamin cleared his throat loudly and we all turned our attention on him. "Uh, I may know someone who can help."

"Who?" I asked desperately and let Lottie help me to my feet.

He seemed hesitant. "A man I once knew. Back where I came from, where I was raised in the Caribbean."

This was all news to me. He didn't even have an accent of any kind. Ben had lived for decades and I never imagined his life before he was imprisoned aboard his brother's ship. Then a disappointing thought occurred to me.

"Ben," I said in a huff of defeat. "That was a hundred years ago. There's no way anyone you knew then would still be alive now."

The corner of his mouth curved upward in a nervous grin. "Well, this was no mere man. He was, uh, immortal. A ghost at times. He dealt with souls and possessed the key to the underworld."

"How can you be sure you can find him?" I asked. "After all this time. Do you even remember his name?"

"Oh, believe me, this was a man not easily forgotten. His name," Ben sighed and stepped forward, "was David Jones."

THE END

Continue the epic tale of Henry and Dianna's adventure with book six in The Dark Tides series, **The Cursed Sea**, available wherever books are sold!

ABOUT THE AUTHOR

#1 International and *USA TODAY* Bestselling Author, Candace Osmond was born in North York, ON.
She published her first book by the age of 25, the first installment in a Paranormal Romance Trilogy called The Iron World Series.
Candace is also one of the creative writers for sssh.com, an acclaimed Erotic Romance website for women which has been featured on NBC Nightline and a number of other large platforms like Cosmo. Her most recent project is a screen play that received a nomination for an AVN Award. Now residing in a small town in Newfoundland with her husband and two kids, Candace writes full time developing articles for just about every niche, more novels, and a hoard of short stories.

Connect with Candace online! She LOVES to hear from readers! *www.AuthorCandaceOsmond.com*

THE IRON WORLD SERIES
CANDACE OSMOND
IRON & WINE
BLOOD & BONE
LOVE & MAGIC
GET BOOK ONE FOR FREE WHEREVER eBOOKS ARE SOLD!
FROM BESTSELLING AUTHOR
CANDACE OSMOND
AVAILABLE WHERE BOOKS ARE SOLD

PAPERBACK
NOW AVAILABLE
THE DONOR
CANDACE OSMOND

KILLER
ME
candace osmond
GUARDIANPUBLISHING.CA
AVAILABLE WHEREVER BOOKS ARE SOLD!

SILENTLY INTO THE NIGHT
"WHAT WOULD YOU DO IF THE MAN YOU LOVED WAS DESTINED TO REAP YOUR DYING MOTHER?"
A NOVEL FROM BESTSELLING AUTHOR
CANDACE OSMOND

WANT MORE TIME TRAVEL FANTASY ROMANCE? CHECK OUT CANDACE'S NEXT SERIES, KINGDOM OF SAND & STARS!